Murder In Key West 10

Edited by
Shirrel Rhoades

ABSOLUTELY AMAZING eBOOKS

Habent Sua Fata Libelli

ABSOLUTELY AMAZING eBOOKS

Manhanset House
Shelter Island Hts., New York 11965-0342

bricktower@aol.com • tech@absolutelyamazingebooks.com
• absolutelyamazingebooks.com

Library of Congress Cataloging-in-Publication Data
Rhoades, Shirrel, editor
Murder In Key West 10
p. cm.
    1. Fiction / Thrillers / Suspense. 2. Fiction / Mystery & Detective / Collections & Anthologies. 3. Fiction / Thrillers / Crime. Fiction, I. Title.
ISBN: 978-1-955036-67-2, Trade Paper

January 2024

Murder In Key West 10

10-Plus Murder Mysteries
for the 10th Anniversary Edition
of Key West's Favorite Anthology

Murder and Mayhem
In Paradise

Edited by

Shirrel Rhoades

The pen is mightier than the sword, they say.
But what about weapons ranging from flare guns to spear
guns to a coconut?
You'll find them all in this murderous anthology.

Here's to those who plot such murders –
mystery writers!

Introduction

1. Dead End
Robert Coburn

2. Calm Before The Storm
Bill Craig

3. Four Fingers
and the
Dead Drag Queen
Shirrel Rhoades

4. The Go-Fast Boat
David Beckwith

5. What's the Buzz?
Randy Becker

6. Walter the Weirdo's
Interrupted Sleep
H.L. Osterman

About The Authors

Introduction
to the
10th Anniversary Edition of
Murder in Key West

Hard to believe, but this is the 10th Anniversary Edition of the Murder in Key West anthology, a decade of collecting short mysteries by writers who have captured the flavor of this southernmost city in the continental United States.

Some of the authors in this book are new, but many will be familiar to those who like to read about Key West, located at the tip of the Florida Keys. It is an island known for its history of pirates, smugglers, sponge fishermen, and tourism. The 8-square-mile spit of limestone sand has been home to such colorful writers as Ernest Hemingway, Tennessee Williams, Thomas McGuane, Annie Dillard, Shel Silverstein, James Leo Herlihy, John Hersey, Richard Wilbur, John Ciardi, Stuart Woods, Robert Stone, Phillip Caputo, and Judy Blume – to name a few.

And you can add the names in the following Table of Contents. Key West is the scene of murder and mayhem in their creative minds. Enjoy sharing their unique tales of Cayo Hueso – the Island of Bones.

-Shirrel Rhoades
Key West

1. Dead End

Robert Coburn

The call came in at 0845.

"This is Sergeant Pete Grant. There's a dead body in the cemetery."

"I'm not surprised," Detective Mike Beasley said.

Beasley worked homicide at the Key West Police Department.

"Isn't it a little early for jokes, sergeant?" he asked. "I haven't even finished my first cup of coffee."

"It's not a joke, detective. I'm at the cemetery. The DB is off Palm Avenue between Violet and Laurel Streets."

The twenty-acre fenced-in Key West Cemetery is divided by named avenues and streets, with a city of gravesites situated between them.

"You know where the naked woman is?" Grant asked. "The victim's there."

A memorial stone near the border fence on Angela Street depicts a naked, bound woman. Smaller foot-stones repeat the same design. Little is known about it.

"All right, I'm on my way," Beasley said.

~~~

"Big hullabaloo happening over there," Iggie Iguana commented while sunning on the broken cement cover of one of the many collapsed graves in the cemetery.

"And it started out to be such a lovely quiet day," Yolanda Iguana mourned, crouched beside him. "I was just there myself earlier. I hate it when people come in here being so noisy. It's enough to wake the dead."

The two lizards shared the space below the cover, a practice not uncommon in the Iguana community in the cemetery. However, some graves were treated more as second homes by those who preferred to occasionally roost in the trees, determined by the temperature, of course. On real chilly nights there was always the danger of passing out and falling from a tree, which in some cases could be fatal.

"It'll probably get worse," Iggie said. "We'll get no peace."

"Well, maybe we can have some fun if it does," Yolanda said with a smile, though you couldn't have told.

"Yeah, we'll freak 'em out," Iggie said with a rascally grin, though you couldn't have told. "I've got a new trick we can pull. Stay still until they get really close, then take off like a bat out of hell."

"Oh, those are fast!" Yolanda giggled. "I'm so glad you decided to move back here from that house, Iggie."

"It got lonely being under there all the time with no friends," Iggie said, a lump forming in his throat. "Although the man who lived in the house did hand out nice treats."

"Well, you're much better off being here with me," Yolanda told him, "treats or no treats. I hear Gabi and Bert aren't too happy since they moved to the Bight even with all the treats they get from the restaurants, poor babies. So there's a lesson to be learned."

"Too close to the water for me," Aggie shivered. "That rain last night was bad enough. Here comes another car."

~~~

A uniformed officer stationed at the cemetery's main gate directed Mike Beasley to First Avenue, which is right below Palm Avenue and was open for him to drive down. Yellow tape had been strung across the entrance to Palm Avenue and on the crisscrossing streets up to Laurel Street, which was also taped off. He parked there and walked to the crime scene.

Sgt. Pete Grant met him.

"So what's the story here, Pete?"

"Patrol was driving past the cemetery earlier this morning and a groundskeeper ran out and hailed them down. Said he'd found a dead body and was going to the office to report it when he spotted them. Weird coincidence, huh?"

The body laid stretched out on its back, an apparent gunshot wound in the right side of the head at the temple.

"Anyone touch him?" Beasley asked.

"No, sir,"

Beasley wouldn't bet on that he thought, bending down for a closer look.

The man appeared to be in his late sixties. He had grey hair tied back in a ponytail and was dressed in jeans and a nondescript shortsleeved shirt, a pair of scuffed Nikes on his feet. He was soaking wet.

"Could be a suicide," Beasley said.

"Haven't found a gun," Grant told him.

"Did the groundskeeper work in this area yesterday?"

"I didn't ask him."

"Find out, would you? Might help to know how long this poor guy's been here."

People had begun to gather along the cemetery's boundary fence on Angela Street. Some were taking pictures with their phones.

"We better have a uniform move that crowd before this thing turns into a circus," Beasley said. "Also, I'll want to canvas those houses on Angela to see if anyone heard or saw anything suspicious. I'll call the coroner."

~~~

Iggie and Yolanda had moved from their sunny slab to the cooler environs of their den below ground. It'd gotten too hot for them and since reptiles can't regulate their body temperature like mammals, they have to take other measures.

"Whew!" Yolanda said. "It's going to be scorcher today. What do you think all that's about up there?"

"Might have something to do with that guy last night," Iggie said. "Walking around here looking at everything after the cemetery closed. I got tired of watching him and went to bed."

"And was I ever glad you did," Yolanda said with a naughty smile, though you couldn't have told.

~~~

The coroner had arrived. The body had been moved during his initial examination, which had given Beasley a chance to look for some identification. He'd found the man's wallet. And a set of house keys.

"John B. Goode," he read from a driver's license showing a photo of the deceased. "Homestead address. I'll get on the horn with the department up there to notify any family."

He put the wallet and keys in an evidence bag.

"So what's your opinion on this being a suicide?" he asked, turning his attention back to the coroner. "Haven't found a gun yet."

"Well, that's certainly a possibility," the coroner said. "Single entrance wound. No exit, so the slug's inside his head. Sign of burns around the wound. The rain probably washed away any traces of powder residue. Couldn't be cleaner if he'd taken a shower. Kind of a bizarre happenstance on that. We'll check for residue, though. His clothes, too. Might be a speck in the fabric. Okay to take him?"

"Yeah, go ahead," Beasley said.

The coroner's assistants put the victim in a body bag and loaded him into the van. Beasley and Grant watched as they drive away.

"The coroner thought it was bizarre that the rain washed away the gunshot residue," Beasley said. "I call it unfortunate. But check this. According to the victim's driver's license, his name is John B. Goode and he was born in 1958. Are you ready?"

He effected a little drum roll, then continued.

"Chuck Berry wrote and recorded Johnny B. Goode in 1958. Now I'd call that bizarre."

"How do you know stuff like that?" Grant laughed.

"My old man was a rocker back in the day. I got a solid education in rock and roll from him."

~~~

Two uniformed policemen were left to search for the gun while Beasley canvased the houses on Angela Street. Three of them were vacant, most likely second homes or vacation rentals. Of the ones that were occupied, he came up empty-handed. Everyone in them had battened down for the storm and had heard only the rain.

Since Five Brothers was only a block away on Southard, Beasley decided to walk up and get a cup of Cuban coffee from Eddie.

The two officers continued the search for a gun.

"There are lizards in this damn place," one said nervously. "Hope we don't see any."

~~~

"What do you suppose those people are looking for?" Yolanda asked.

She and Iggie, having reached a comfortable body temperature, had returned to the top of their slab. In fact, the day had cooled somewhat due to a northwesterly breeze and it was beginning to cloud over. A possible shower might be in the making.

"Whatever, I hope they'd find it and leave," Iggie said.

"When I was over there earlier this morning I ran across something strange wedged in the rocks," Yolanda said. "Maybe that's what they're trying to find. You'd never see it from where they are."

"Maybe they'll give up then and go home."

~~~

Beasley returned to the police station and called the Homestead police department. The two officers continued the weapon search at the cemetery for another hour before deciding to try again in the morning. Palm Avenue remained cordoned off. The rain never did materialize.

~~~

Dayshift had just completed roll call when Beasley got to the station. He'd been up half the night thinking about the case. So many what-ifs and how-comes. Not to mention nothing making any sense.

He settled at his desk in the detectives room and phoned the Homestead police department to follow up on his notification request. He got the sergeant he'd originally spoken with.

"Yes, Detective Beasley, we sent two uniformed officers to the address. It appears the man lived there alone. They asked a neighbor and he confirmed it. Said he didn't know if there was any family. We'll get a court order to enter the residence once we have a death certificate."

"Thank you very much, sergeant. Appreciate your help."

"Any time, detective."

More pieces to a puzzle that doesn't fit the picture, Beasley thought after hanging up. Then another thought. Did John B. Goode have a past he wouldn't have wanted known? Wouldn't be the first person. He decided to run the name on NCIC, the central database for tracking crime-related cases. And he got a hit.

Indeed, John B. Goode had been convicted of assault with a deadly weapon.

Contacting the arresting agency, he learned that the assault had been on a woman and the weapon had been a piece of rope tied around her neck.

The image of the naked bound woman on the memorial stone at the cemetery flashed in Beasley's mind. Followed by a crazy idea.

He checked his watch and then went to the evidence room.

~~~

"Help me with this stupid thing," Yolanda said.

"How about I get on the other side and we both push it up with our noses," Iggie suggested.

They were in a small crevice between some broken pieces of concrete.

"Okay, I'm ready," he said. "Let's do it."

And working together they finally flipped the small automatic pistol out of its hiding place and into an open area.

~~~

Three hours later, Beasley arrived in Homestead. His GPS led him to the street and the address. He parked in front of the house. Getting out of his car, he saw that no one was around. That was good. He mounted the steps and opened the front door with the keys that'd been in Goode's pocket. Before stepping inside he slipped on a pair of gloves. Though he had the keys, he was still breaking and entering. Better not to leave any fingerprints.

The living room was sparsely furnished. Off it was a combination kitchen and dining area. A hallway led to a bathroom and two bedrooms. The first had a king-size bed that nearly filled the room. The second one wasn't furnished for sleeping. It was equipped for kinkiness.

A simple cot with a thin mattress sat in the center of the room. A length of scarves knotted together to make a rope curled on top. Numerous sex toys were tossed about. A rack of sorts with wrist-ties and ankle-ties stood against one wall. Paraphernalia that he could only imagine the uses for sat around on the floor. But the most startling of all was a framed sketch hung on another wall.

Its subject was a naked, bound woman.

~~~

Iggie and Yolanda had just emerged from their den when the police car stopped. They quickly scampered to the top of the slab.

Two uniformed officers got out of the car and walked toward the scene.

"This is going to be good," Yolanda said excitedly. "How long do you think it'll take them to find it?"

"It's in plain sight," Iggie said. "Unless they're blind."

Yolanda thought the idea of a blind policeman was funny.

"Your friends are waiting for you," one of the officers taunted good-naturedly, motioning toward the lizards.

His partner suffered from herpetophobia, a fear of reptiles. It'd been his luck to draw this assignment.

Iggie and Yolanda had moved to a higher point on the slab to get a better look.

"Those fucking things are so creepy," the other officer said with a shudder.

"Did you hear what he called us?" Iggie asked. "Fucking things!"

"I wish you wouldn't use that kind of language," Yolanda told him.

"I've a good mind to run over there and give him a piece of my mind," Iggie said.

"Well, he was rude," Yolanda agreed. "I did find it offensive."

And with that, Iggie hopped off the slab and ran toward them. Like a bat out of hell.

"Christ, he's coming right at us!" one of them shouted.

The other one turned to run but tripped over his feet and fell.

Iggie stopped short.

"Shoo! Shoo!" the other officer yelled at him, waving his hands.

Iggie calmly strolled away.

"You okay, pal?" the officer asked his partner.

"I'm alright" he said, "but you won't believe this."

He pointed at the gun lying on the ground where he'd fallen.

"How did we miss it?" he asked in exasperation. "I swear we've been over every damn square inch of this place a hundred times."

"I'm calling the sergeant," his partner replied, "then we're out of here."

Iggie and Yolanda shot each other high-fives, being careful not to lock their sharp claws together.

~~~

Beasley was only a few miles out of Key West but his mind was still in Homestead.

He'd risked his job and possibly more by going there. And what had he learned? John B. Goode was heavy into sadomasochism. Did that have any connection with his death? He couldn't say. There was the drawing of the woman. Where did it fit in? Was guilt involved? Enough to commit suicide? Or was there revenge? Strong enough to commit murder. Questions only he can ask himself because he can't discuss this with anyone.

His phone rang. He put it on speaker.

"Hey, Mike, this is Pete Grant. Thought you'd like to know we found the gun."

~~~

The slug recovered from John B. Goode's brain matched the gun. Another piece of evidence was his fingerprints on the bullets remaining in the magazine. The death was ruled a suicide.

~~~

Iggie and Yolanda crouched side by side on the top of their grave cover, taking in the last of the sun. The yellow tape had been removed earlier that day and the people were no longer around. Soon the cemetery would be closed for the night. They finally had the place to themselves.

"This is the best," Yolanda said dreamily.

Iggie replied with a satisfied grin, but you couldn't have told.

2. Calm before the Storm

Bill Craig

Hurricane warnings were normal in the Florida Keys and Key West was no exception. Rick Marlow had weathered a couple already. Things had been unusually quiet on the rock. The island's economy was just starting to recover from the Corona Virus pandemic and the tropical storm that had proceeded it. Rick was in the office by himself, his cousin Greg, a recent addition to Marlow investigations, was busy on a case that had taken him to Miami.

The door to the office opened and a young man walked in. He looked like a typical spring-breaker type, bleached blond hair, dark tan, wife-beater tank-top, and cargo shorts. The kid looked a little uncertain, but that was nothing new for somebody looking to hire an investigator. Most folks were never sure what to expect, given the television shows and movies.

Not to mention the fact that Rick looked like an old beach bum more than a private investigator. It was a look he had started cultivating when he had first come to the island from being a cop in New York City. "Can I help you?" Marlow finally asked.

"Are you Marlow?" the kid asked.

"I am. You are...?" Marlow left the question open.

"What? Oh, yeah, sorry. My name is Ted Fielding. Uh, my girlfriend Josie, she disappeared last night."

"What do you mean, disappeared?" Marlow asked.

"We were at a party on the beach. Sure, we had been drinking, but nothing harder than beer," Ted explained.

"You're sure about that?"

"I swear to God," Ted raised both hands in supplication.

"So, you were at a party on Smather's Beach...?" Marlow prodded.

"Yeah, and Josie had to go to the bathroom. So, she walked back to the parking lot and disappeared. She never came back and after a while, we all started looking for her. She was nowhere to be found," Ted explained, a glum expression on his face.

"Did you check where she had been staying?"

"Yeah, but she wasn't in our room. She hadn't shown up by this morning and the cops won't do anything. They blew it off as her being a flake."

"You have a picture of her?"

"Yeah," the kid replied as he pulled out his phone and pulled up a picture of a vibrant-looking red head with blue eyes and a scattering of freckles. Marlow had the kid send it to his phone. Knowing what she looked like would make hunting for her easier.

"I 'll want five hundred dollars a day plus expenses. And if I find her in less than five days, I'll give you four hundred back."

"You seem pretty confident that you can find her quick."

"I know the island. That's why you came to me."

"I just want to know that she's okay," Ted shook his head.

"I'll find her, Kid, don't worry," Marlow assured him. The kid put the money on the desk and Marlow wrote him a receipt. The kid gave Marlow a picture of the missing girl and then left.

Marlow studied the picture for a few minutes. Josie really was a beautiful girl. Maybe just a little too good looking to stay with a guy like Ted. It was something to think about as he hunted for her.

Marlow headed out the door not long after his client had left. He headed for Duval Street. There were people there he could talk to. If they had seen Josie, Marlow would find out. Something about the case wasn't sitting right. He just couldn't pin it down.

After touching base with some friends who kept an eye out for him, Marlow would head to the police station to talk to the Chief, Jamie Gutierrez. Marlow had to admit that he was curious as to why the cops had blown Ted Fielding off. Maybe they had felt that something was off with the man's story as well.

~~~

Jamie Gutierrez groaned when he looked up and saw Marlow standing in the door of his office. "You got a minute?" Marlow asked.

"Not really, but I don't suppose you'd pay attention to that answer," Chief Gutierrez replied. He nodded to the seat across from his desk. Marlow dropped easily into it. The two were friends and had saved each other's life more times than either could count.

"I had a guy hire me this morning to find his girlfriend who vanished from a beach party last night."

"Ted Fielding. Yeah, I figured he'd go to you."

"His story smells," Marlow offered.

"Yep, like a frightened skunk. I think he knows more about her disappearance than he's letting on," Gutierrez replied.

"I agree. I'm still going to look for her, and if I find her and he's dirty, I'll bust him for you.

"If he's dirty, call me. Don't start going all vigilante on him."

"Would I do something like that?'

"Right," Gutierrez rolled his eyes. Marlow grinned at him and stood and walked out. Leaving the Chief grumbling behind him.

~~~

The sky was clear and the temperature was hot as Marlow walked out of the building. It was early afternoon and the streets were filled with tourists. Despite Covid and hurricane damage, Key West was bouncing back. Teens and young women in the barest of bikinis and flip flops were taking advantage of the warmth and sunshine to enhance their tans and attract the eyes of young men in board shorts and wife-beater tank tops. There were a few families interspaced among the throng of people, but they were far out-numbered by the youngsters. Josie Grace was out there somewhere. Marlow intended to find her, no matter what it took.

Marlow headed for Duval Street. He had people that he needed to talk to. People that would put the word out about Josie Grace. They would let him know if they heard anything. If Josie Grace was not being held, Marlow would know soon enough.

If she was being held, Marlow would know that too. Right now, he wanted to do a little more digging into Ted Fielding. Something about the guy just didn't ring true. Marlow had his doubts about Josie Grace being his girlfriend as well.

It didn't take long to get back to the office and Lola Loomis, his secretary/office manager/partner was installed behind her desk. Marlow had worked for her late husband, Walter Loomis, and Marlow and Lola had become friends. Lola had been Walter's secretary as well.

"New client?" Lola asked when Rick walked in.

"Yeah, but I'm not sure I buy the client's story. He hired me to look for his girlfriend who allegedly disappeared from a party at Smather's beach Friday night."

"Did he go to the police?" Lola asked.

"Yeah, but Jamie didn't believe his story either."

"So what are you going to do?"

"Can you do some digging on this Ted Fielding for me?"

"I can."

Marlow thanked her and headed for his desk. He had a few things that he wanted to check on his own. His first call was to Jim Westin over at the combined drug interdiction task force. Marlow had a suspicion that Ted Fielding might be known to Westin.

~~~

Two hours later, Marlow as at the home base for the Joint Interagency Task Force. While Westin claimed otherwise, Marlow was pretty damn sure that the man was a CIA-backed spy. His cousin Greg had confirmed his theory for him a few months back.

"Ted Fielding, you said?" Westin asked, a frown wrinkling his forehead. Marlow pulled out his phone and pulled up a photo that he had stealthily snapped of his client and turned the screen so Westin could see it better.

"Yep," Marlow replied laconically.

"You have a picture of the allegedly missing girlfriend as well?"

"I do. You recognize her?" Marlow asked.

"Agent Lauren Killian, Drug Enforcement Administration. She dropped off the grid a week ago. She was bringing in intelligence about new routes that the Columbians are using to smuggle cocaine into the states. Your client, Fielding is an enforcer for the Serosa Cartel. If he is looking for her, she is in serious trouble."

"I figured as much. You guys want Fielding?"

"We do."

"Then how about I give him to you, and maybe find your missing DEA agent as well?" Marlow asked.

"Tell me more," Westin said.

~~~

Marlow returned to the office knowing more than he had when he had left. It was after five and Lola had already left for the day. Sitting at his desk, Marlow booted the computer and entered his case notes. Once he had finished, he took a few minutes to read it over. One thing was clear. He would find Josie Grace, but not for Ted Fielding. He fully intended to take Fielding down, one way or another. For a moment, he wished that Greg was around for this one, but he was busy in Miami. So, Rick would have to handle this one on his own.

To do so, Marlow would have to crawl into Agent Josie Grace's headspace. She was a DEA agent on the run from a Cartel hitman. Key West was not a big place, being an island. So, where would she go to lay low? She hadn't gone to the local police or to JITF offices. That meant she had some kind of bolt hole on the island. All Rick had to do was find it.

Marlow stood up and headed out after locking the office. He missed the old office that had been in a house that had belonged to Walter Loomis, his former employer and also the man that had saved his life. Sadly, the house had been blown up by Cartel hitmen, the same ones that had shot him and had cost him the rest of his left lung. Greg had caught them and taken them out and then insisted on sticking around and becoming a partner in Marlow Investigations.

Smather's Beach was the last place that Josie Grace had been seen according to Ted Feilding. Marlow wasn't sure he wanted to give the man that much credibility, but it was a place to start.

Marlow unlocked his bicycle from the rack in front of the office and headed for Smather's Beach. He suspected that Josie Grace had a bolt hole near there. He had to try and find out.

Smather's Beach was nearly deserted when Marlow arrived. All but a few hardliners had already left for Mallory Square and the nightly Sunset festival that was a big draw not only for tourists, but also for the locals. He locked his bike in a rack near the Southernmost point in the United States marker.

He had an uneasy feeling and was glad that he had his Ruger ECS 9mm in a pocket holster in his shorts pocket. The sun was sinking in the west and gentle swells were rolling in off the Gulf of Mexico. There were still a few die-hards out in the water, but most were heading to the beach because dusk was a prime feeding time for sharks in the tropical waters.

He was glad to see that they were smart enough to not want to feed the local sharks. Marlow trudged through the sand keeping an eye out for any woman that might be Josie Grace. There was one young woman, her head covered by a wide floppy hat and large sunglasses that obscured most of her face, she was wrapped in a large towel. She was glancing nervously around, obviously afraid of something.

Marlow dropped to the sand, sitting so that he could look out over the water and yet keep the young woman in sight in his peripheral vision. He suspected that he had found the woman that he was looking for, but he wanted to make sure.

Ted Fielding had gone to ground as well. Marlow had requested that Key West police department pick the man up. He had vanished from his motel and disappeared without a trace. That didn't set well with Marlow. It confirmed his impression that there was something off about his client.

She glanced around repeatedly and furtively. It was obvious that she was looking for someone. Marlow figured enough was enough, so he got to his feet and started walking in her direction. He kept his pace slow so as not to spook her. He remembered that she was a trained agent that had been deep undercover for nearly a year. He had no desire to make her nervous, but he had to let her know that he could be trusted.

The girl looked at him when he dropped onto the sand to sit beside her. "Do I know you?" she asked.

"Not personally no. My name is Marlow and I'm a private investigator. Do you know a man named Ted Fielding?"

"Shit," she whispered, her eyes going wide and her face went pale.

"Relax. Jim Westin from the JITF told me who you are. He asked me to bring you in. Fielding is a cartel hitman and he actually hired me to find you, using the old missing girlfriend dodge."

"So, are you working for him?" Her voice was tense.

"Not since I found out that you are undercover DEA trying to get back in," Marlow replied truthfully. Josie breathed a sigh of relief.

"I need your help. That Fielding guy was sent to kill me. Can you get me to Westin?" Josie asked.

"I can and I will," Marlow assured her. They both stood, brushing the sand off the seat of their pants as they started for the parking lot. Suddenly, they were bathed in the ultra-white glare of digital headlights.

"Gotcha!" yelled a familiar voice. Marlow reacted, shoving Josie out of the light and snatching his pistol from his pocket and wiping the safety down with his thumb, raising and firing at the lights. One headlight exploded and Marlow dived for the darkness outside the shaft of light.

Fielding fired back, his bullets digging furrows in the sand. Except Marlow was no longer there. Running in a low crouch he had darted thirty yards to the right and had run and darted up and through the brush that separated the beach from the road. Feilding was visible in the backlight from the remaining headlight. Marlow raised his gun and fired twice. Fielding spun, his gun flying away before he fell to the ground.

Sirens were sounding in the air as Marlow ran forward. Fielding was dead. Josie came stumbling out of the shadows, one hand clutching her right shoulder. Blood was running down her arm. Marlow pocketed his gun and tore off his shirt, using it to staunch the bleeding. Marlow pulled out his cell and called Jim Westin. "I've got your agent. We at Smather's beach."

3. Four Fingers
and the
Dead Drag Queen

Shirrel Rhoades

Wharton Dalessandro was straight as a stick, but he liked to go down to the 666 Club on Sunday afternoons for Gay Bingo. It wasn't the game that attracted him; it was the spectacle.

There was something about these flamboyant drag queens – the exaggerated femininity, the dazzling clothing, the bawdy humor, the societal defiance – that entertained him. They were part of the cultural mosaic that made people call Key West by the etymological sobriquet "Key Weird."

Bingo took place on the club's second floor, a large cabaret where nightly drag queen performances took place. A raised platform served as stage. The lead performer was Saphra, who was Queen Mother for the club's ragtag troupe of dancers, singers, and comedians.

For bingo, a table was placed on the stage. On it sat a rotating cage filled with numbered ping-pong balls. Behind it hovered the game's host calling out the random numbers. A drag queen known as Twinkie, she was noted for her large Carmen Miranda hat decorated with bananas and tropic fruit. From time to time between calls, Twinkie would peel off a yellow banana and eat it suggestively.

The expansive room was filled with narrow tables for the players. The participants fell into three groups: Local gays, a table reserved for local straights, and an assortment of tourists who were "walking on the wild side." The local straights wore T-shirts that jibed: PLEASE DO NOT TEASE OR FEED THE STRAIGHT PEOPLE.

The audience liked Twinkie for her snappy patter, having trained the local customers to give trained responses to each number she called out.

"10? That's how many boyfriends you had last month, Twinkie."
"3? That's the length of your twinkie, Twinkie!"
"42? That was your age ten years ago, Twinkie!"

Twinkie didn't mind being the butt of the jokes; it was part of her shtick.

However, it was no joke when Twinkie keeled over dead. Her Carmen Miranda chapeau had tumbled to the floor, bananas scattering like giant yellow commas.

Wharton Dalessandro, being a retired New York City cop, stood up and shouted, "Everyone stay in your seat till the police get here!" He was already dialing Police Chief Johnny Leigh's private number on his iPhone 13 Pro.

Pressing his fingers against Twinkie's carotid artery, he determined that the bingo caller was dead. And judging by the long nail file sticking out of the back of her neck, it was clearly murder. Heart attacks didn't come with a metal shiv piercing the brain stem.

Twinkie's birth name was Alexander Martin Carmichael. Even though being a drag queen, Alex had maintained that he had no desire to actually be a woman. "I'm a gay performer," he used to say. "This is just a costume. The first time I ever dressed as a female was when I was hired to play Daisy Duck at Disney World. Blame Walt Disney for my career direction ... oh, never mind, Governor DeSantis will!"

Drag queens came in "many flavors," Twinkie had explained. "Gays, trans, titty queens who had surgery in order to look like a woman. The whole gamut."

When Twinkie wasn't hosting Gay Bingo, she performed a cute "Little Mary Sunshine" number on Tuesday and Thursday nights. For this, she swapped the Carmen Miranda hat for an umbrella prop. She skipped across the stage, singing and twirling her blue parasol to the audience's delight. On the other nights, she worked as an escort for out-of-town visitors. By "escort," she didn't mean tourist guide.

But that was no more. At the base of the nail file, blood trickled down Twinkie's neck like a ruby necklace. The crowd was murmuring uncomfortably. Flashes lit the stage as people used their smartphones to record the scene for posting to their Facebook accounts.

A slender blonde in a cheerleader costume was wailing loudly, trying to get to the stage, but was being held back by fellow drag queens. Wharton recognized her as Twinkie's partner, Lulabelle.

They shared a century-old conch cottage over on Thomas Street in Bahama Village. She was clearly distraught.

"Calm down, girl," ordered Saphra, who had come from behind the stage's back curtains. "You're scaring the tourists."

Lulabelle tried to stem her sobs, but ended up issuing a series of hiccups.

The Queen Mother patted her on the back, while holding tightly to one arm, restraining her from approaching her partner's body. "There, there," she murmured reassuringly. "What's done is what's done."

For several years now, Saphra (né Ralph Ray Morrison) had been one of the dominate drag queens on the island – an icon on a par with Sushi, Chris Peterson, Randy Thompson, and Inga. People often referred to her as "the toughest bitch ever squeezed into a sequin dress." She was known for her gruff manner and flashy attire.

Just then, the Police Chief and his entourage came stomping up the stairwell. "Hey, Four Fingers," he called Wharton Dalessandro by his nickname, derived from a missing digit on his left hand, "you phoned in a murder."

"Over here," the retired NYPD detective responded. "It's Twinkie."

"Shot? Stabbed? Bludgeoned?"

"Stabbed – a nail file in the base of the brain."

"How'd it happen?" Chief Johnny Leigh asked, his coppery countenance reflecting his Hispanic heritage. The heat of the night left his face slick with sweat.

"We were playing Sunday bingo, Twinkie calling out the numbers, doing her usual patter, when the lights flicked off. Thought nothing of it, the power grid being unstable here in Old Town. When the lights came back on a minute or two later, Twinkie was slumped over the table, dead as a speared hogfish."

"Anybody see who did it?" interjected Sergeant Clifford Weeks. He was a fat, pig-like man, not very popular with his fellow lawmen. Rumor had it he took bribes.

"How could we?" said one of the club's performers, a singer who called herself Jenny Wren. "The lights were out, you idiot."

"Hey, watch your mouth."

"Eat a kielbasa," shouted a diva known as Trixie Rainbow.

"Listen you –!"

Chief Leigh spoke up. "Everybody settle down. Somebody in this room is a murderer. Nobody is going home till we figure out who killed Twinkie Twatsie."

"How are you going to do that?" said Saphra. She was wearing a sleek cocktail dress covered with sequins. She paid fellow drag queen Sushi to sew her costumes.

"My friend Four Fingers here is gonna do it. He has a knack."

"Whoa," said Wharton Dalessandro, holding up his hand like a stop sign. That emphasized his missing finger. Rumor said he'd lost it in a gun fight, but he kept saying it was a fishing accident. "I'm just a private citizen. These days I paint houses, not solve crimes."

"C'mon, pal. You have a rep for being able to finger a murderer in four minutes or less."

"A figment of your imagination, ol' pal."

"I've seen you do it."

"I was probably drunk."

"Solve this one and I'll buy you four beers."

"Make it five."

"Deal."

Four Fingers Dalessandro turned and pointed to Ralph Ray Morrison. "Saphra did it," he said.

"Hey, where do you get off accusing me?" shouted the Queen Mother.

"You were jealous over Twinkie's popularity. Rumor was Club 666 was going to promote him to your spot. So you killed him."

"Prove it."

"Well, those glittering nails you have take a lot of care. That big nail file belongs to you. While it's not engraved, if you look close one can see your initials – RRM – scratched on the handle."

"So it's mine. Somebody stole it."

"No, you were backstage during the bingo game. All by yourself. That's where the fuse box is. You cut the lights long enough to step from behind the curtains and jab him. What we have here is a fatal unilateral vertebral artery stab injury leading to bilateral cerebellar and brainstem infarction."

"Huh?"

"That's a new dress, isn't it?"

"Right. Sushi delivered it just this afternoon."

"Those sequins provide the final evidence. Look at that stage curtain, you can see black sequins sticking to the red felt fabric where you pushed through it when the lights were off."

"They probably brushed off when I came out after the lights came back on."

"No, you came out from the side – Stage Left, I think they call it."

"Okay, I did it. No way was I going to let that fat buffoon replace me as host of the nightly revues. I'd heard the rumors. If I had to do it over, I'd stab her again. Nobody pushes Saphra aside."

Police Chief Johnny Leigh turned to his sergeant. "Clifford, read Saphra her rights and take her into custody. I've got to buy Four Fingers a few rounds of beer."

Wharton Dalessandro looked down at his bingo card. "Too bad," he muttered. "I was just about to call out 'bingo!'"

4. The Go-Fast Boat

David Beckwith

Coast Guard Lieutenant Boggie Gordon's radar showed another craft approaching at a high speed in Hawk Channel while his Coast Guard cutter was on routine morning patrol. Suddenly he saw a 50-foot blue cigarette boat streaking across the horizon. He looked through his glasses. It was the usual fiberglass deep "V" racing hull he had seen many, many times. He estimated its speed at 50 knots. There was no name. He could see it carried a four-man crew. "No illegal aliens," he thought. It did fit the profile of a drug smuggling boat, however. He decided to look into it. He called the boat and its position into his ground base. He instructed his pilot to swing around and contact the boat by radio to inform the crew the Coast Guard wanted to inspect it.

The go-fast boat continued to approach the cutter but showed no signs of slowing. Gordon instructed his radio operator to once again order the boat to stop and cut its engines. It continued to approach full throttle. Becoming alarmed, Gordon ordered his Agusta MH-68A Stingray chopper for assistance.

The go-fast boat momentarily slowed. When it did, Gordon saw that one of the men aboard appeared to be holding a rifle. But then instead of stopping, the renegade vessel reaccelerated and almost rammed the cutter. At the last second, its captain jammed his boat into a hard starboard move, missing the cutter by no more than thirty feet. Gordon's gunner fired twice over the bow, purposely missing the boat. The man with the rifle fired back. The blue strobe light on the chopper came on. The chopper mission commander gave some blips with his siren and on his loudspeaker ordered the boat to stop.

The blue boat instead streaked by and headed towards Looe Key, the protected underwater marine sanctuary three miles away. The cutter swung around and tried to maneuver itself into position to pursue. The chase was on. Gordon cursed. He knew if the smuggler chose to go through Looe Key, civilians could be in danger. He thought the go-fast pilot must be nuts. What were the odds he could negotiate through the Looe Key reefs at a high rate of speed without hitting something or someone? When the boat was in the middle of the Looe Key sanctuary, it suddenly stopped. Gordon could see men hurriedly throwing bales overboard. He had been right. These were drug smugglers.

Suddenly Gordon heard rotors overhead for the backup he had requested. The "Little Buddy" chopper had arrived. The smugglers heard it too. The lightweight, twin-engine helicopter approached the boat and again ordered it to kill its engines. The renegade captain instead suddenly jammed his boat into gear. The boat shot forward. One of the smugglers lost his balance and fell into the water. He screamed insanely as the go-fast props caught him, severing his head from his body. Red was suddenly everywhere like there had been a shark attack. Gordon could see the horror on boaters' eyes as they started comprehending what had just happened. "Shit! I can't try to disable the boat with all these people around and risk hitting an innocent person."

The rogue pilot never slowed down or looked back except to make a "U" turn and make a run back through the diving and snorkeling area, the chopper following. Gordon slowed the cutter momentarily and ordered one of his men to retrieve one of the bales. When the bale was aboard he confirmed it was cocaine. Other packages were bobbing and drifting in every direction from one end of Looe Key to the other.

The coke runner's boat suddenly stopped again. The man with the rifle now was holding an AK-47, which he sprayed at the helicopter. The chopper executed a defensive maneuver. The sharpshooter sprayed him again, getting lucky, this time connecting, wounding the pilot with a ricocheting bullet despite his KEVLAR vest. Shit! The helicopter gunner still couldn't shoot. There were head-boats full of tourists out for a diving adventure who screamed in horror and panic over the invasion taking place in the protected underwater sanctuary. The co-pilot tried to maintain control of the chopper as he assessed the extent of the pilot's injuries. The blue go-fast boat headed for open sea, leaving the bloody scene behind. Almost appropriately, the severed head of the smuggler bobbed up behind a dive head boat causing a fat, hysterical, middle aged woman to puke, faint and fall overboard dragging a part-time dive instructor into the water with her.

"This ain't going to play well in my report or in the press," Boggie Gordon thought.

5. What's the Buzz?

Randy Becker

It was hot. Shirt stuck to your body hot.

The awnings were up. The windows were open. It was that kind of day.

Any breeze struggled through the screens. Inside the air was hot metallic. Everything felt heavy.

The old shack was not much more than a shanty. It sold bait. It sold basic groceries. For the right person, it also sold drinks.

To the one side a ruddy road ran by. On the other side was the slight rise of the train tracks.

You know the place.

About 25 miles north of Key West. Only through way down there on those tracks.

The road passed by from the north but didn't leave the island to the south.

Mangroves. A strip of land. Lots of water. Lots of mosquitoes. A small dock gulf side.

Had been a busier place. Once even a stop for the train. That was before '29.

Not much passed by now. One or maybe two trains a day. Glamor gone from them too. Dingy old coaches. No more fancy observation cars. Barely any freight.

Still, he listened. Listened for the distant sound of steam and whistle.

Today there was only silence. No, wait. There was a buzzing. Not mosquito buzzing but something more insistent.

Once heard the buzzing could not be ignored.

It had a ferocious bite to it.

Stumbling off his stool behind the counter, he went to the window and peered out. He could hear it better but could not see it.

Opening the door meant letting in more of the heat. It faced the afternoon sun.

Opening the door meant, maybe, letting in some of the noise. Or what was making that noise. No screens on the door.

He opened and then shut the door in one swift motion. He was suddenly outside.

Sun beating down. Humidity beating him up. And the buzzing. That damn buzzing.

He followed his ears. Down the side path, the one that led between the road and the tracks. The way to the outhouse. Man, did that shithole stink in this weather.

But the buzzing wasn't there. It was further into the scrub. Past the few struggling palmettos. Past the patches of swamp grass.

Figured if he had gone this far, he might as well go all the way.

The buzzing grew louder. More insistent. More concentrated.

Now he knew what it was.

Flies. A whole swarm of the big-headed ones. The noisy, bitey ones.

So many they began to create shadows in the sunlight.

And then he saw it. What the flies had seen, or smelled, or sensed, long before.

A body. A dead body. A woman's body.

Fully clothed. Almost fancily clothed. Too hot clothed for the afternoon.

Too dead for dying this afternoon.

Lying all wrong. Like the doll his sister had once had. The doll he had broken just to annoy her.

Finally, the smell rose up to match the buzzing. Overwhelming.

The piled-up rotting sargassum had nothing on this.

Gagging. Deafened. Skin-burning ... escape.

Inside again, breathing deep. Gifting himself with a strong drink.

What to do?

No telephone. Nearest one about a mile north along the railroad. Long, hot walk.

Not likely anyone would come by on a day like this.

But someone had to know. Someone had to do something so the buzzing would end. Some had to do something for that poor lady out there.

He would wait an hour. Sun going down some. Maybe a breeze would come up.

But could he wait the hour. Could he stand that noise of death out there?

Going for help would mean leaving that noise. Yes, get away from it.

The door slammed behind him. No need for a lock out here.

Train track or road? Neither offered shade.

Walking the tracks was harder. Who knew what slept under those sleepers?

Road. Dusty. Empty. Long.

But soon enough the buzzing was behind.

~~~

The boat slid easily alongside the dock. Sheriff's deputy knew the knots.

The sun almost to the horizon.

He showed the deputy where to look. The deputy already knew. The buzzing was still there.

But why?

The deputy saw only a matted expanse of tall grass.

Dark stains of blood.

Flies, buzzing flies.

No body.

The man's story had once been true. Not any longer.

A breeze would take the flies away. A sudden rain would wash the blood into the sand and marl. The grasses would seek out the sun again.

But nothing could erase what he had seen.

~~~

The next boat load was more than human.

The barking pair of hounds needed no coaxing. They wanted land. They wanted that smell.

Against strained leashes, they dashed forward.

Making right for that place. Scattering flies in their wake.

Noses to the ground. Blood sniffed. And again.

A few yelps of pained awareness.

Paws moving quickly, through the grasses. Past the outhouse. Only a short sniff there. Beyond the shack. Out across the road again.

Onto the dock.

Their energy stopped. They lay down. No more hunt in them. No more scent.

The deputy shook his head. Dead end trail. Water's edge.

Looking out over the flats, the deputy just shook his head. No point even thinking about it.

The body was gone.

Loaded up his dogs. Gave a wave bye. Set out, back to his home dock up the Keys.

~~~

A man out on the water. Night falling. Lots of thoughts come to him.

Whose body had it been?

How had she died?

Why was the body there?

How had it gotten there?

Fallen off a passing train?

Pushed off a passing train?

Or somewhere, somehow else?

Why was the body gone?

The old bait-seller couldn't give much of a description.

The noise, the smell, the body's brokenness. All blocked any other awareness.

No mention of wounds. No gunshots. No knife marks. Just broken. Like a doll.

Blood, yes. But from what?

Nothing to go on without a body.

Have to wait to see if anyone is reported missing.

Look at the stars. Steer by them and familiar mangroves.

A fattening moon was rising making that easier.

Return home.

~~~

Evening's breeze ran true. It dispersed a few of the flies.

Sleep would not come. Not only because of that damned noise.

Continuing to see too much. Not through his eyes.

He could not stop his thoughts.

He could stop those flies.

Scooping up buckets of water at the dock. Crossing the road of marl. Moonlight bleaching the marl white where his buckets slopped.

Drenching the spot where she had been. Washing away the blood. Washing away the scent. Giving the flies no reason to swarm.

Bucket after bucket.

Feeling better for doing something.

Feeling better for cleansing the spot.

Feeling better for the growing silence.

Feeling better ... what is this?

A small bauble, a brooch.

Too shiny to be there long.

Too shiny to be old.

Too out-of-place to have ever been there before.

He would take it up to the Sheriff in the morning.

But now, silence. Cooler night. Breeze. Sleep.

~~~

Calm water. Bright moon. Far from mosquitoes.

Peace.

Until almost at the dock.

Hounds suddenly awake. Alert.

Then howling. Eager.

At the dock, straining to sniff the dock.

More howls. Following a trail.

Off the dock. Into the parking area.

To an empty spot.
Tire tracks of today.
Then nothing. Dogs lying down. Nowhere to go.
Another dead end.
No, not a dead end.
Back to the dock.
Dog tired of it all but going anyway.
Back to where they had tied up.
But now going out the dock.
Noses alert again. Leashes strained again.
Past skiffs.
Past yachts.
Until the deeper water end. Out where the sailboats tie up.
Dogs fully engaged now.
One great leap.
One is in a dinghy behind the *Albatross*.
The other howls encouragement from the dock.
The deputy plays his light on the dinghy.
The moon supplies any other light needed.
The dinghy is clean.
Too clean.
Nothing docked here for long is this clean.
Boats washed clean are never really clean.
Too many places for dregs to hide.
The deputy knows this.
The hounds can smell it.
The body has been here.
It came from there to here.

It went from here to a car.
He knows whose car it might be.

~~~

It is very late.
The yard is fully moonlit.
The house is dark.
The car is parked carefully in its usual spot.
The dogs are very interested in it.
The deputy is very interested in it too.
His knock awakens nothing.
He knocks again at the front door.
A light toward the back flickers on.
A voice asks what it is.
Sheriff's Office.
The expensive door groans open.
Greetings.
A few questions.
A few answers.
Good night, sir.
Good night, officer.
Now, more questions in mind.
Will have to wait until morning.
Long day.
Too late.

~~~

Thank God, it is overcast.

One can feel a line moving in.
He is up from a fitful sleep.
Too many dreams to count.
The brooch is right where he left it.
On the top of the table by the bed.
In the back room.
Not much to call home.
But, in these days any place to call home is home.
No coffee this morning.
Too much to do.
Brooch in pocket.
Heading north by the road again.
Nothing buzzing anywhere.

~~~

Thank God, it is overcast.
Weather change coming.
The deputy is up from a fitful sleep.
Want to get things done before it rolls in.
No coffee this morning.
Notebook filled with questions and some answers.
Phone calls need to be made.
Another trip out to that house.

~~~

Thank God, it is overcast.

Weather change coming.
He is up from a fitful sleep.
No coffee this morning.
Too many questions were asked.
Need to get a move on if he is to be moving on.
Leave the house.
Take the car?
No!
Walk to the dock.
The back way.

~~~

The deputy is at his desk.
Phone calls have been made.
Time to follow up on what he now knows.
As he opens the door, the bait-seller is just reaching for the knob.
The brooch shines in the daylight as much as it had in the moonlight.
It has been seen before by the deputy.
In a picture in *The Citizen*.
In the society section.
Outside a house he had visited only a few hours before.
On the lapel of the wife of the owner of the *Albatross*.

~~~

Two people heading for the same place.
One on foot, along the back way.
One by car, along the road.
Into the parking lot.
Backing into a space at the rear of the lot.
Seeing the *Albatross* still at dock.
No sail unfurled.
No sign of life.
A sudden motion.
Someone walking the path by the water.
Checking if he can be seen.
Walking toward the dock.
Siren.
A mad dash onto the dock.
A quick scramble.
No match for the fit deputy.
Cuffed.

~~~

Trial was short.
Evidence was simple.
Testimony about the body.
The found brooch.
The hounds' trail.
The missing wife.
Too many holes in his story.
His story.

He and his wife had traveled by train to Key West.
She was off to Cuba for a vacation out the island.
Not able to be reached.
He had returned by train home.
He had gone fishing.
Gutted the fish in the dinghy.
Dragged the bag of fish guts to his car to use as chum.
But holes, too many holes.
All in rebuttal.
No ship leaving Key West showed her on its manifest.
Train conductor remembers couple boarding going south.
Also remembers them both boarding in Key West.
Icily sitting in separate seats.
Didn't see either detrain.
Figure they had only ridden part way back to where they had started.
Lots of folks do that to visit friends.
No fish guts found anywhere on the property.
Brooch was purchased by the defendant.
Several vouched for her always wearing it.
But then the clincher.
The old Florida East Coast Railway.
Losing money. Cut back services.
(Not like it once was!)
Car cleaners only working every few days.
"Lost and Found" held what they found.
And there, in the jumble of the found -

Found by the side of the door of the baggage car shuttling back and forth to Key West -

One lost shoe.

The shoe she had been wearing in that photo.

By that house.

Before she had threatened to leave him.

Before he had gone with her to Key West to try to talk her out of it.

Before she said she was done.

Before he ....

~~~

Her body was never found.

His days were short.

Before the gallows could swallow him, he became his own hangman.

~~~

Every once in a while, when the dry season is too long, the buzzing begins again.

Out there.

Between a through highway from Miami and the abandoned railroad right of way.

No remnant of any old shack.

No dock.

The flies swarm where blood is still in the sand.

6. Walter the Weirdo's Interrupted Sleep

H.L. Osterman

Walter de Worchester was homeless – but if you were going to be living without a roof over your head Key West was certainly the place to do it. The weather was wonderful, soup kitchens plentiful, and cops were mostly friendly. Summers are hot and winter is warm. The highest recorded temperature in Key West is 97°F; the lowest is 41°F. And there are pleasant sea breezes.

Lately, Walter has been camping out in a dead-end alley behind a mailbox store off North Roosevelt. The cops had arrested him for trespass, but being an ex-lawyer he had pointed out that this was public property and he had a right to be there like any citizen. Charges were dropped. It wasn't worth the court's time to deal with the finer points of his argument.

The judge, the arresting officer, the police chief – heck, almost everybody on the island – knew Walter. He was a colorful character, somewhere on the autism spectrum. Sort of a Rain Man. He had helped solve several local murders to Police Chief Sam Marrero's chagrin.

People called him Walter the Weirdo, an apt description.

Walter was on the waiting list for an apartment in Paradise Plaza, a subsidized housing complex off Duck Avenue. He was number 1,212 on the list. So for now, a sleeping bag in the alley would do.

That's how he came to discover the dead body.

Walter woke up at 6:21 a.m. at the first ray of sunshine. "Move over," he mumbled, tugging at his sleeping bag.

His brother was always hogging the bed.

Then he remembered that he hadn't seen his brother in 50 years, when they were kids in Wisconsin. Those cold winter mornings always invited a struggle over the blankets.

So who was snuggled next to him? Certainly not Willie, his younger sibling.

"Excuse me, but –" He paused when he saw the lump piled at his side. A man he didn't recognize. The man, given his waxy gray pallor and rolled-back cloudy eyes, was most definitely deceased.

"Yikes!" he screamed, jumping up, clutching his fleece-lined sleeping bag tightly to his shallow chest. He fumbled for his glasses, put them on to get a better look-see. Most folks recognized him by his round Harry Potter glasses and sweeping mustache and black bowler hat. This morning the bowler hat was perched on the head of the dead man.

John Pike, owner of the nearby Mailbox Marketplace, came racing over. He had been unlocking his front door, arriving early today to begin an annual inventory. "What's going on over here?" he shouted through the thick bougainvillea trees to his itinerate neighbor.

"A d-dead body," pointed Walter.

"What the hell –?" said John Pike, dialing 9-1-1 on his iPhone. "Did you kill him?"

"No, of course not. I've not even been introduced to this gentleman."

"You don't have to know somebody to kill them."

"It would be rude to murder a stranger!"

Walter the Weirdo was one who minded his manners.

Officer Carlos González was first on the scene, followed shortly by Chief Marrero. A few passersby had stopped to rubberneck.

"Did you kill this man?" Chief Marrero asked Walter.

"Of course not," the little man replied. "And I can prove it."

"Oh – how?"

"By identifying the culprit."

Sam Marrero crossed his arms. He was a 5th-generation Conch, meaning his family had lived on the island since the days of wreckers and pirates. Sam's great grandfather had been one of Porter's anti-pirates Mosquito Fleet. Now Sam was eradicating latter-day pirates – mainly burglars, bicycle thieves, and drug dealers. "Okay, Walter. Do your magic. Solve the crime for me."

"If you insist," he said, looking around at the gathering crowd. Among the gawkers were a few recognizable faces. Archie Cunningham stood at the front of the onlookers. He was owner of the Holiday Tiki Bar, a tourist watering hole on the Bight. And next to him was Phil Brandenburg, a well-known insurance agent. In the back was Howdy Handleman, a desk clerk at Blue Water Resorts.

"Looking at the dead man, I'd say he was a tourist. Tommy Bahama shirt, Bermuda shorts, but the white untanned skin is the giveaway."

"That's right," spoke up Howdy Handleman. He checked in at Blue Waters last night. I was working the desk."

"Did he go out after checking in?"

Howdy nodded. "Said he was going to do the town. Left around 8 p.m. Didn't come back. I was on duty till 6. I'm on my way home."

"I can vouch for that," Archie Cunningham spoke up. "I spotted him drinking at the Tiki Bar last night. He was pretty loaded."

"Was he by himself?" asked Walter, squinting his eyes at the florid redhead.

"Seemed to be."

"I know this man," offered Phil Brandenburg.

"How so?" interjected Chief Marrero. His interest piqued. He pushed his cap back, exposing his brown forehead to the morning sun.

"I sold him a million dollar life insurance policy yesterday afternoon just after he rolled into town. A big score for me. Don't get too many walk-in customers like that."

"And how come you happened to be here this morning?"

"I was out celebrating last night too. But with my girlfriend." He indicated a slender blonde standing next to him. She looked pretty woozy, the victim of a long night of drinking and revelry.

"Thaz right," she slurred.

"Name?"

"Nancy," said Brandenburg.

"No, I mean the dead man."

"Stewart Willingham. From Boston, as I recall."

Chief Marrero turned to Walter. "So who killed Stewart Willingham?" It was more a taunt than a question.

"Easy peasy," smiled the little man, retrieving his bowler hat from the dead man's head. "It's well known that murderers often return to the scene of the crime. That means the perpetrator may indeed be standing here among us, checking in his handiwork."

"Hey –!" growled the Tiki Bar owner.

"No me," whined the desk clerk.

"I have an alibi," the insurance agent pointed to his girlfriend.

"No, none of you," Walter assured them. "I regret to say the murderer is none other than my neighbor John Pike here."

"Wait a minute," protested the mailing outlet owner. "You can't prove that."

"How do you come to that conclusion?" interceded Chief Marrero.

"What are the facts?" shrugged Walter. "Stewart Willingham is a tourist from Boston. He arrived in town yesterday, bought an insurance policy, went out on the town, got sloshed."

"Hey, who was beneficiary of that million-dollar policy?" asked the chief. Seeing this as a way to head off Walter's beating him to a solution.

"His mother," said the insurance agent. "He just sold his business, wanted to take care of his 87-year-old mom."

"Back to why you say John Pike killed him," sighed the chief.

"He didn't mean to kill Stewart Willingham. It was a case of mistaken identity. He meant to kill me."

"You?"

"I regret so. Mr. Pike has been complaining about me camping here next to his shop. Says it's bad for business."

"That's true," said Officer Gonzolez. "John Pike has made numerous complaints. Just yesterday he. Told me if the police didn't do anything, he would."

"Poor Mr. Willingham had been out drinking, was on his way back to his hotel. Blue Water is just up the street. But he needed to pee so he ducked into this alley."

Chief Marrero frowned. "How do you know that?"

"You will note that Mr. Willingham's Bermuda shorts are still unzipped. And that jocund bush over there is wet. When he spotted me, he picked up my bowler hat and tried it on – the way drunks might do. John Pike came out here to do me in, saw a man in a bowler hat and thought it was me. So he stabbed him with a letter opener. You can see it there between his shoulder blades. It has the Mailboxes Marketplace logo on it. *Quod erat demonstrandum*," he concluded.

John Pike seemed to slump. "It was still dark. I saw that bowler hat and lost it. Who would care if some homeless bum died on the street. It would look like a mugging."

"Jeez, John. I've gotta arrest you," apologized the police chief.

"Key West needs to do something about these homeless people," grumbled the mailbox manager.

"Oh, one thing before you take him in," Walter the Weirdo piped up. "Can he mail this letter for me? It's another application for housing at Paradise Plaza."

7. Accounting In Paradise

Steve McMillan

I'm an accounting professor at Temple University in Philadelphia. My long-time girlfriend, Sharon Levin, is a homicide cop. We've been involved with murders in Philly, New Orleans, and the Outer Banks, among other locales. We've been chased by killers internationally in Malta, Belgium, and Finland. While there have been very different circumstances across these adventures, one thing has remained constant: We have never been accused of killing anyone.

Until now!

Sharon and I have had many good things happening of late, including moving in together in the Rittenhouse area in downtown Philadelphia. We had helped uncover a mob connection to the ultra-Orthodox Jewish community. We assisted in exposing a gambling group that was involved in the death of a New York Giant football player. In short, things have been pretty decent lately, but we were both tired. We decided it was time to take a quick trip. Spring Break was coming up for me, and Sharon had some time coming to her. But we weren't sure where to go.

We discussed several places but realized we had never been to Florida besides Disney World. Tampa looked nice. Miami has all the art deco area. We even discussed going back to Disney because there was a lot that we had not seen. But in the end, we decided on Key West. We thought Key West looked great, so we pulled the trigger on a trip.

My Spring Break was in mid-March this year, which according to all our research, was an excellent time to go. It will still be pretty crowded, but the weather will still be reasonable and not unbearably hot.

I had made some extra money with the Aramark case and the football player, so I decided to splurge. At first, we would fly to Miami and rent a car, but we only had five days, so I paid for the flight to Key West. I even splurged for first class. I got us a room in one of the more extravagant hotels, The Heron House. I had even done some research on restaurants and bars. When you only have five days, you must use your time well.

We had flown into Miami from Philly and caught our flight to Key West. We were in first class, too. Sharon turned to me and said, "First class all the way Stone. Aramark must have done you well."

"Not bad. And we are in first class, so is it time to try the mile-high club?"

"Short flight, so maybe not, but the hotel you picked looks great. We can pretend we're on a plane back at the hotel."

"Works for me!"

We landed at the Key West International Airport. We were used to traveling light and only had our carry-on luggage. A lot of Uber possibilities, but we decided to take a cab.

When we got to the hotel, we were both very impressed. The hotel had a great pool, greenery, and a magnificent hotel room for us. As soon as we got to our room, we decided it was a great time to start our trip with a mile-high moment—actually, a moment or two.

We took a quick nap and then headed out. I had already made a dinner reservation for us at Bagatelle at 8 pm. We knew the Mallory Square Sunset Celebration started at about 6:30, so we went in that direction.

Once we got there, we were very impressed with everything happening. We saw magicians, local musicians, a tarot card reader, various jewelry, art, and painted seashells. We took many pictures and asked some people to take some pics of us.

While walking, I noticed a young guy hanging out near the water. I couldn't place him, so I asked Sharon. "See that young kid over there with the Phillies hat on? I can't place him, but he seems familiar. Do you recognize him?

Sharon looked and said, "Nope. I don't think I know him. But you do see a lot of students, so maybe he's one of yours."

"Maybe. I guess it doesn't matter because he doesn't recognize me either."

After spending a little more time watching the festivities at Mallory Square, we made our way to Bagatelle. The menu had many food choices, but I had read about the lobster mac and cheese made with Caribbean spiny lobster. We thought that we should get the mac and cheese and something else to split, but we saw someone near us with the mac and cheese. We smiled and decided to get two portions of the mac and cheese. Two rounds of the best food around seemed the best way to go.

It was almost 10 pm before we finished dinner, and we were both tired even after our naps. We took one more stroll around the center of town and then headed to our hotel. We weren't even interested in a nightcap when we got to our room. We just toppled into bed and out like lights.

The following day, I was up before Sharon. It was almost 11 am, so I got some coffee and found a Key West Citizen newspaper. I bought a newspaper as a souvenir because I assumed there would be an online version of the Citizen. I figured I'd get some information about some more things in the Conch Republic.

Once I returned to our room, Sharon was up and waiting for her coffee. She said, "Can't believe I slept so late. Rarely do that. Thanks for the coffee, Ben."

"No problem. Let's have some java, grab showers, and then we'll figure out what we want to do today. Still interested in the Ernest Hemingway House and Museum?"

"Gotta see those six-toed cats! Can I go first in the shower? I need to take a Hollywood one. Stand in the water."

I smiled and said, "Take your time. I'm going to glance at the local news online.

While I sat back to read the news on my laptop, the headline caught me. **Local fisherman killed near Mallory Square.** A murder occurred around midnight, not far from our hotel.

Based on the story, it sounded like someone had struck a fisherman on his head, or as they say in some of Sharon's cases, death by blunt force trauma. I read the whole story and felt sorry for what happened, but I kept reading the news.

Just as Sharon stepped out of the bathroom, there was a knock at the door. Sharon went back into the bedroom, and I opened the door.

Two men in police uniforms were standing outside our door. One said, "Hello, my name is Officer Eastman, and my partner here is Officer Little. Are you Professor Ben Stone from Temple University in Philadelphia?"

"I am he, but how could you possibly know that?"

Eastman replied, "Because one of our residents says he saw you kill a man about midnight this morning. We need to come in." With that, they started to step into our room.

I stood for a minute to block their way but decided I was outnumbered and had done nothing wrong. I let them into the room.

Sharon came out fully dressed and said, "Officers, did I just hear that you think Dr. Stone somehow murdered someone earlier today?"

Officer Little said, "Yes, Ma'am. There was a report that Dr. Stone bludgeoned a man to death around midnight."

Sharon smiled and said, "Let me reach into my pocket, please." She did and pulled out her badge and opened it. "Gentlemen, as you can see, I am a member of the Philadelphia police department. I can assure you that Ben had nothing to do with what happened with the murder."

Little said, "Maybe so, but my Chief would like you both to come into the office so he can ask you some questions. He needs to know where you were last night, and can anyone corroborate that?"

I knew that meant that Sharon was going to now blow a gasket. She said louder, "Are you two fucking kidding me? I'm a homicide detective. You can see the badge. We're happy to answer questions; I'm a cop, so I know how it goes, but we won't be treated like suspects."

Eastman replied, "Detective, our Chief wants to talk with you. We are not making any accusations **at this time.**"

Sharon leaned over to Eastman and said, "Which suggests that you might make accusations later. I've spent a lot of time meeting with possible suspects, so I know what "**at this time**" means. Let Dr. Stone get dressed, and we'll get this straightened out with your Chief."

I said, "I'm fine dressed like this. Let's get this over with."

The officers put Sharon and me in the back seat of their patrol car. No one said anything, but Sharon and I just held hands. Once we arrived at the precinct on Roosevelt Boulevard, we entered the office, and Eastman asked us to sit in the chairs next to the door. We did as we were asked.

I could tell that Sharon was starting to fume. She's been in many stations other than hers, but she had never been in one where one of us was a possible suspect of a crime. I tapped her shoulder and said, "Try to stay calm. Let's get this done."

"I'll try to keep it together, but if this Chief starts insinuating that you killed a guy, he will get an earful. Maybe even a kick to the nuts if I can get to him."

"Let's try not to get arrested."

After about fifteen minutes, Eastman waived us to come in. We walked into the office and saw the Chief sitting behind a desk. The Chief had a similar uniform as the cops did, but he had some silver hanging down on his shoulders. Clearly, he wanted to make sure that everyone involved with the police in Key West knew who the boss was.

He said, "My name is Chief Smith. Please have a seat."

Sharon and I sat down next to Smith's desk. The two cops stood behind us. Smith said, "I just want you to know that my first impression is that you didn't kill that guy last night."

Sharon said, "Well, that's a good start, Chief. However, then why are we here?"

"Because first impressions aren't the only impressions. I want to hear how things went down last night for you two."

I could tell Sharon was getting hotter, so I jumped in. "Well, Chief, Detective Levin and I came down for a few days in Key West. We arrived yesterday afternoon. We're staying at the Heron House. Last night we went down to Mallory Square for a while, then we had dinner at the Bagatelle. We walked around for a few minutes after dinner but were back at our hotel by 10:30. We went to bed, and neither saw nor heard anything while in our room."

Smith said, "So that's it?"

Sharon jumped in and said, "You're damned right; that's it. But I want to know how Dr. Stone got involved in this in the first place?"

"One of our locals, a kid named Rick Porter, called 911 last night and said he saw Dr. Stone kill a guy last night."

Sharon said, "And that's enough for you to haul us both in for questioning. Because a kid says, he saw Ben kill someone. That's bullshit, and you know it."

The Chief replied, "No, I don't know, it's BS. And if you were in my shoes, you would have to have some answers and not just pretend nothing happened. I have a suspect, and I need to follow up."

Sharon started to say something, but I knew she was angry, so I tapped her shoulder and said, "Well, what we said is all we have. We didn't leave our room until this morning; no one saw us last night. I don't know what else we can do."

"I have one detective here who is looking for any clues. He is examining for anything that might indicate what happened. But until we figure out what might have happened, I must ask that you don't leave the island."

That sent Sharon off. She yelled loudly, saying, "So you are considering us suspects. Are you fucking kidding me?"

"Detective, since you are a member of law enforcement, I'm going to let that outburst go. But it would be best if you calmed down. We're just doing our jobs."

"No, you're not doing your jobs because we told you what happened last night, and we had nothing to do with the death. This is total and complete bullshit."

The Chief said, "As I said, I'm giving you the benefit of the doubt, but you need to get yourself under control, or I will have to take other actions."

Sharon replied, "And what other actions are you threatening us with?"

The Chief said to Eastman, "Officer, please put Dr. Stone in cuffs and escort him to our holding cell. Perhaps law enforcement in Philly doesn't play by the rules, but we do. I gave you plenty of leash, and you used it all."

With that, Officer Eastman came from behind me and broke out his cuffs. Sharon stood and started interceding, but the Chief said, "Detective, if you make a move, I'll have you in cuffs, too."

I turned to Sharon and said, "Don't do anything right now. Try to find a lawyer down here who can get me out on bail. Then we'll figure it out."

With that, I put my hands behind my arms, and Eastman cuffed me. I said to Sharon, "Don't worry, honey. I'll be fine. Just find a lawyer."

I spent the night in a detention facility over on Stock Island. They gave me food and water, and I could use the bathroom. I even got a little sleep.

At about 9 am, the Chief came into my cell at the detention center, coupled with Sharon. As best I could tell, Sharon had not smashed him in the balls, so that was probably a good thing.

The Chief said, "You are released, Dr. Stone, but you are still not to leave the island. Detective Levin made quite the ruckus last night, but there isn't an attorney on the island right now. I released you based on her good faith promise that you two won't leave. I promised Detective Levin I would keep her apprised of what was happening."

I said, "So we should pretend that nothing happened and continue our vacation?"

This time Sharon tapped me and said, "Let it go, Ben. We'll be fine. Let's go."

We left the precinct and got an Uber to ride back to our hotel. I began to say something, but Sharon hushed me and said, "Don't start talking until we're in the room."

When we got into our room, Sharon said, "Sorry, Ben, but I think we will have to investigate independently. Key West is a small place, and I feel that the Chief and the rest are leaning towards believing the local kid, Rick Porter."

"I agree. What should we do?"

"I think we should take a chunk of cash from the ATM and start spreading it around downtown. See if any info jumps out."

I said, "Let's do it!"

We withdrew the max from the bank, $500. Then we decided to walk around the fishing area, Garrison Bight, and chat with any locals around. At first, no one seemed to have much to say, but finally, a fisherman told us that Porter works on a fishing boat and will probably be back in port around 5 pm. He also gave us our first real clue: he said Porter was from Philadelphia and moved down to Key West about a year ago. The fisherman also told us that Porter works on the Riptide boat.

We set up surveillance by the dock and watched as the boats started coming in. We waited for Riptide to enter the port.

At 5:30, we saw Riptide heading in. We saw it tie up, and the day fishers disembarked first. Sharon asked one of the guys standing next to the boat if he knew Porter. She offered him 20 bucks to tell her when he saw Porter. About 10 minutes later, the guy points out Porter, and Sharon gives the guy the 20.

Sharon points out Porter to Ben, and he says, "Wait, now I recognize him. He was at Temple and took my intermediate accounting class. I remember him because he flunked my class and came to my office to complain. He was furious that I had ruined his academic career, at least in his mind. I tried to tell him he could retake the class, but he never calmed down. I had to ask him to leave my office. Never had that happened before."

Sharon said, "Then I think we must tell the Chief what we've found."

We went back down to the precinct and asked to see the Chief. Once we entered his office, I said, "Chief, I recognized the kid who accused me of murder. He is one of my former students, Rick Porter. He flunked my class and lost it in my office."

The Chief said, "You're sure?"

"Very sure."

Sharon said, "So, Chief, now you have a clue. You need to check in on this Porter kid."

"I know where Rick lives, so I'll ride to his house. He lives in a small place over on Stock Island."

"Since I'm a homicide cop, I will ask you to take us with you.

The Chief agreed, and the three took his patrol car to the house. Once they got there, the Chief knocked on the door, but there was no answer. However, they heard movement, so the Chief opened the door. They saw Porter packing up a duffel bag.

The Chief asked, "What you up to, Rick? Where are you headed?"

Porter replied, "Just taking a little road trip, Chief. Looking for better places to fish."

"Really? Are you sure you're not running away because you killed a guy the other night?"

"Hell, no, Chief. Why would you think that?"

"Because Dr. Stone here seems to recognize you from taking classes at Temple in Philly. Apparently, you weren't happy with one of your grades."

Porter looked like he was thinking about running, but the Chief shook his head. "It's an island, Rick. You know you can't get away."

Porter turned to me and said, "I flunked out of college because of you, you asshole."

I said, "One class doesn't flunk you out. You must have had some other bad grades."

"Maybe so, but your class is what did me in. If not for you, I would be a practicing CPA, making a lot of money, and not be pushing boats around down here."

I said, "I'm sorry that your career got short-circuited, but was it worth killing a guy?"

"It was to me."

The Chief said, "Well, I hope it was. Rick, you are under arrest for murder. Put your arms behind your back."

Porter decided not to resist, and the Chief took him into custody. He turned to us and said, "I'm sorry for your night in the detention cell. Pick a restaurant, and I will pick up the tab."

Sharon said, "Thanks, Chief, but we'll pay for our own dinner. I think you overreacted a lot during this whole thing. I'm just glad we cleared this thing up."

The Chief said he had to take Porter in his cruiser, but he said he would come back to pick us up. Sharon was still pissed with the Chief and said we would get back on our own.

We got an Uber ride to take us back to our hotel. Once we got there, I ordered two margaritas, and we sat out by the pool.

I asked, "Well, I'm glad we got that behind us. What do you want to do now since we have a couple of more days?"

Sharon smiled and said, "Don't know about the next couple of days, but I think a mile-high event would be appropriate after this drink."

"Don't have to ask me twice!"

8. Always Count on Greed

Renee Kumor

A land of sunshine, sand and ocean is a foreign country to a Minnesota boy. Yet here he was, invited because of some obscure relative. He and a half dozen other strangers had inherited something from some guy. Casey Handel didn't know the guy. Maybe the others did. When he had gotten the attorney's letter he had called his Pop. He was the only one alive. Mom had died a few years back and her only brother years before, leaving no cousins, or any kind of blood kin. After all these years it was just him and Pop, and whoever Pop could remember as kin.

Casey reviewed the letter from memory. The attorney said it was one of Mom's cousins. He had never been introduced to cousins. Mom and Pop had met in Vietnam. He was in the infantry and she had enlisted as a nurse. She only enlisted after she learned that her only brother had been declared MIA. She never admitted it, but Casey was certain she had gone to Nam to find him. But by the time she got there, his body, decaying but still with ID tags, had been found. She stayed to help save the wounded. That was Mom, a nurse twenty-four/seven.

His parents had reconnected years later and he was their only child. That's why Casey knew there were no other relatives in Mom's family. Mom's brother never came home. Everyone else had died years ago. Or so he thought.

Then he had received the attorney's letter. He was informed that he, along with five others listed in the letter, was an heir to an estate in Key West, Florida. The letter came with a travel voucher, hotel reservations, and a request for information to verify identity. One of Mom's cousins had left an estate and he was one of the heirs - in Key West, of all places. In February!

Casey Handel was a well-trained law enforcement officer in his mid-thirties, single, as in divorced, no kids, no cousins and no entanglements. A few years ago he had suffered several almost lethal wounds, but modern medicine and his own tenacity kept him alive and brought him back to ninety per cent of his former physical strength and ability. He was finally standing erect and painless at his six-foot height. That wasn't enough for his old department. Medical retirement became his future.

But that didn't end his law enforcement career. He was now a professor, teaching basic law enforcement classes at the community college and criminology classes on the local campus of a respected university. As several friends had teased he was the new heartthrob professor on campus - tall with that Minnesota Scandinavian look. But he didn't have time to charm co-eds. He carried a full class load at the university and taught at the community college in the evening. With both jobs and his retirement pay he seemed to have more income that he had ever had, but Pop's care ate up a lot of it. Ah well, you do what you gotta do.

His watch burped. Time for the meeting with his cousins and the attorney.

The law office was very professional. Even in the sunshine and sand world Casey was impressed with the organization and attention to detail as he entered. A brisk older woman nodded to him, asked his name and compared his name and photo to the list on her desk. He gave the attorney a lot of credit for making certain each heir had provided proof of identity as well as the photo. He would have asked for fingerprints and a DNA sample. He smirked. Yeah, he'd want that if he were solving a murder. This attorney just needed to give away some money.

He was ushered into a large conference room that looked ready for business. A big monitor hung on the wall and drinks and snacks covered a credenza at the side of the room. And, of course, the obligatory windows brought in all the sunshine, sand and ocean. Three strangers stood at the windows. They turned as he entered. A woman broke away from the group and walked toward him extending her hand. "I'm Taylor Waterman, and you are?"

He took her hand, marveling that the attorney, Taylor Waterman, was a beautiful woman, tanned, slim, sun colored hair and maybe early thirties. This will be an interesting weekend, thought Casey. "Ma'am, I'm Casey Handel."

"It's a pleasure to meet you, Mr. Handel." She turned to the others in the room. "I'd like to introduce Mr. and Mrs. Ross. You and Mrs. Ross are heirs to the Douglas Faraday estate. We're waiting for three more heirs to join us." She swung an arm toward the refreshments. "Help yourselves. I'll go collect the others."

The heirs studied one another. "Did you know Mr. Faraday?" asked Mrs. Ross. She was older than Casey. She and her husband looked about sixty. They were both dressed in what Casey thought of as Key West business attire - light fabrics in solid soft colors. "I've asked my mother and her siblings but no one remembers this man. Ms. Waterman says I'm related through my father's uncle." She stared out the window, seeking an answer. "Dad's been dead for years and he never said he had rich relatives."

"I told you, Sybil," said Mr. Ross. "I've researched the attorney and this Faraday. Everything is on the up and up. We can give whatever we get to the kids. Besides who could turn down a free trip to Florida in February?"

Sybil smiled at Casey. "Henry doesn't expect more than a few thousand dollars. I'm just pleased that our travel expenses are covered. We came from Boston." She looked at him waiting for him to reveal his hometown.

She's a clever interviewer, he thought. "I'm from Minnesota. And I never met Mr. Faraday. I was told I'm related on my mother's side, but she's dead and had no siblings. My pop didn't know she had this relative." The door opened and the attorney led in three other people.

"We're all here she announced. Please help yourselves to some refreshments, then take a seat and we'll get started."

"How long will this take?" asked one of the newcomers.

"We should be finished by noon," Taylor replied. No one said more. They all followed instructions, grabbing a drink and a snack, then finding a seat at the table. She smiled at everyone. "Let's introduce ourselves. Let's start with you, Sybil, and go around the table."

Sybil smiled. And surprised Casey with the poise and ease she showed as she addressed the group. "I'm Sybil Ross and this is my husband, Henry. We're from Boston. Henry owns a property management firm and I work in HR at MIT." She gave everyone a conspiratorial grin. "I'm one of the few on campus not an engineer." The group smiled back at her. She had melted any ice in the room.

Henry nodded and said, "I'm with her." He turned his attention back to a pastry.

The next person introduced himself. "I'm Kenley Taggert. I come from Albuquerque. Been there all my life. Do some ranching. Ain't rich." The man appeared to be older than Sybil by a good decade. He had a weathered look that put truth to his claim as a rancher. "Never met any Faraday."

"I'm Boz Greco." A small, energetic man threw out his arms. "As you can see, I'm wondering how I got invited to this party." Boz was a mixed-race fellow about thirty. And the race wasn't clear. Asian, Native American, Black, or White? Physically it seemed to all be wrapped up in one person. A very compact, handsome person. "You may have heard of me. I'm an actor." Everyone stared, not wanting to admit their ignorance of current entertainers. He smiled. "Well, you really haven't heard of me. But I am an actor." He named some current movies and

two Netflix series. "I'm what the trade likes. A real flexible face."
He smiled.

"I'll have to Google you," Casey promised. He nodded
around the table. "I'm Casey Handel." He shook his head. "I'm
not an engineer, an actor or a rancher. I teach basic law
enforcement at a community college and criminology at a
university. Because of injuries received in the line of duty, I had
to retire from the force."

The man sitting across from Casey and looking bored said,
"I'm Bert O'Keefe. I live up in Miami. And never met Faraday."
He looked at the others, daring them to ask questions. He was
forty-ish, with that Florida glow - both good health and wealth.
"I do a little land development and real estate investment."

Taylor let the room absorb the introductions for a moment.
"I'm Taylor Waterman. I was Mr. Faraday's attorney. As you may
know there are firms around the country who look for heirs so
that we attorneys can close out estates. The company we hired
found all of you. They also found Delores Swing. However, she
had an accident in her car and didn't survive." Taylor ruffled
some papers. "Delores was forty-seven, single, no family and
lived modestly in a small town in Maine as the county librarian.
I spoke to her on the phone when she first received our letter. I
was looking forward to meeting her." There was a silence in the
room as everyone thought about their unknown, deceased
cousin.

"I know you all may be curious about your relationship to
Mr. Faraday and to one another." She patted a folder. "I've
included that information in your packet.

"But let me get on with today's business. Mr. Faraday owned a small isle." Taylor stood. Walking to the window, she pointed. "It's that small group of palms to our left. It is about twenty-five or thirty acres and you all can decide its future. Mr. Faraday refused all offers from developers. In his last years he became a recluse. We only met once a year to deal with taxes and to make certain he had his estate in order." She sighed heavily. "He did have his estate in order but his heir died about eight months ago and Mr. Faraday refused to dictate another will."

"Who was the heir?" someone asked.

"His young housekeeper. She came to Key West fifteen years ago as a run-away. Mr. Faraday took her in and she worked as his housekeeper, secretary, driver, both car and his small motorboat, and anything else he needed."

"Was she his mistress?"

"He never said and I never asked," Taylor replied. "The other attorneys here tell me that once she entered his life he was a new man and when she died, he closed off all contact with everyone."

"How did she die?" Casey was curious.

"She drowned," replied the attorney. "She was down at Mr. Faraday's dock at night. The police think she tripped on some item on the dock and fell hitting her head then rolled off the dock into the water. He found her the next morning." Taylor shook her head. "It was very sad."

Taylor had been standing at the window. She returned to her chair. "As I said, we have verified each of you as eligible heirs. Together you own that isle. My office recommends we organize you all into a corporation. You can then look for a buyer. Or you can all decide to keep it natural and just pay taxes, possibly hire a guard to patrol or a caretaker to live in Mr. Faraday's house. You can each use it as a timeshare, select a time of year and claim it as your own. You can each decide to build your own place and live there permanently or as a second home. The possibilities are endless."

"Can we see this place?" Boz asked.

"I came here in my yacht from Miami," said Bert. "I can take us out there."

Sybil chirped, "I guess we're talking about more than a few thousand dollars apiece. I'd like to see this estate, too." The others nodded.

Taylor cleared her throat. "I thought you all might ask to see the place. I've scheduled a trip for tomorrow. We'll have lunch there and return about four when the launch service has to prepare for evening clients." She turned to Mr. O'Keefe. "Thank you for offering your yacht. The depth around the isle would prohibit mooring at Mr. Faraday's dock." Mr. O'Keefe nodded and asked a few questions. Taylor answered in a seemingly foreign language. Casey guessed it was all nautical talk. He had a boat on his small lake. But it only moved when he rowed. Ocean nautical considerations didn't have meaning on a small Minnesota lake.

Taylor returned her attention to the table. "My firm doesn't expect you all to reach any conclusions this weekend. We want you to get to know one another and see the property. We can then gather, or meet online, in a few months and start addressing the property's future."

Bert stood and looked over the group, then grabbed a bottle of water. "You all come to my yacht this evening. I'm at the yacht club. I'll order up some food and we can get acquainted." With that invitation he gave them an address. Everyone pulled out a cell phone and entered it into a GPS app, then they all exchanged phone numbers. The cousins were gelling.

Taylor said, "What a lovely idea! You'll be on your own. I have another commitment. But before you all set sail, let's get the paperwork completed." With that she presented each heir with a packet of papers and began her explanation of each document. She had been correct. It was noon when they finally finished. "Tomorrow we'll met at one of the tour services." She gave everyone the address. "We leave about 10:30 and we'll return about 4. Bring sun screen and dress casual." She smiled. "This is the Keys. Life is casual!"

~~~

The Friday evening gathering on Bert's yacht was very enjoyable. He introduced two young men as his crew saying he always sailed with a crew just to be cautious. The club provided snacks and drinks. Once everyone was settled, Bert and his crew entertained their guests with a sunset cruise. When they returned Bert docked at a local restaurant with oceanside parking, bragging at his crew's skill at finding a convenient slip. Everyone followed their host along the dock. The island and the family tree report were the topics of conversation. They enjoyed a relaxed evening sharing incredible seafood offerings and getting to know one another.

Of course, Casey, always suspicious, wondered if Bert was softening everyone up for some ulterior motive like development rights or something. But he went back to his conch chowder and forget to be suspicious.

After dinner Boz tried to get up a group to go bar hopping. Obviously the cousins were not party animals because he got no takers. Kenley reminded everyone that he had crossed several time zones and needed to recover before they found him asleep in his dessert. Bert wanted to get his yacht back to his slip at the club. And Sybil Ross just chuckled at the invitation. "Dear," she reminded Boz, "I'm old enough to be your mother." She kissed his cheek and said good night. She and Henry headed back to their hotel.

Casey slapped the young man on the back. "I hate to admit it, but I need my sleep, but I'll have a drink with you, first." They all parted with the promise to meet tomorrow for an exciting visit to their property.

Casey and Boz found an interesting tourist bar that was close to the shuttle stop for their hotel. "Don't you love this atmosphere?" Boz spun around taking in the lights and sun-soaked crowd.

Casey laughed. "It sure is different back home. I won't see this much skin on folks until maybe July."

"Brrrr," teased his new cousin. "I think you should buy me a drink just for helping you thaw out."

And that was how it went. Two cousins talking and sharing a drink. Casey rubbed his eyes, "You can stay but I do have to get to bed. It's been a long time since I stayed out late drinking." He slapped Boz on the back. "You're a bad influence. See you in the morning."

Boz finished his drink and studied the crowd. He always liked to imagine his surroundings as a movie set. He thought about where he would place cameras, how he would work the lighting. His eyes moved from one corner of the room to the other. He stopped, turned his head back to the left. Had he seen someone familiar? He stared. Shook his head. Couldn't be, he thought, that wasn't the plan. He had one more drink and some great conversation with one of the musicians and finally called it a night.

~~~

Saturday morning everyone was on time. "You folks are great," exclaimed Taylor. She was dressed in baggy denim capris, a long-sleeved t-shirt and sturdy lace up shoes. She presented a far different picture than the professional well-turned-out lawyer of yesterday. She smiled at the puzzled faces. "I've been to the island before. It's no paradise, just an overgrown pile of sand.

"I saw trees from your window," said Sybil wondering if her sandals would be a problem.

"Trees, vines, ferns." Taylor waved her arm toward the island. "If it can germinate, it found a home on the island. As he aged Mr. Faraday neglected all but the area around his cottage."

"Wildlife?" asked Casey.

She nodded. "It's a great nesting habitat. Probably some small land critters and the ubiquitous lizards, you know, geckos, skinks, anoles." Someone shuddered loudly at the thought of lizard life on the island.

"Taylor?" called a man climbing from a tourist motor launch, "We're all set. Your lunch was delivered and we've got some coffee and muffins."

"Great, Josh. My folks are all on time." She quickly introduced everyone to their host captain. "Josh is taking us out this morning while the rest of his crew prepares for a 'reservation only' sunset cruise this evening."

"On this?" Bert clearly had a mild distain for the well-used craft.

The captain laughed. "No, this is my doing-a-favor-for-Taylor ship. The paying customers will cruise in style."

The cousins all laughed and teased Taylor for arranging a cruise with Gilligan. But they all climbed aboard in high spirits. Taylor began her guide spiel as they left the dock. "Let me describe the island." She unrolled a large satellite photo of the area placing it on a table in the launch cabin. "It's five miles from the pier to Faraday's dock." Her finger indicated a small structure on the island. "It's on the north side of the island. Here you can see the walkway to the cottage. And it is a cottage. Probably about fifteen hundred square feet. Indoor plumbing, with a septic field. He caught rainwater for flushing and laundry and brought in drinking water. He used propane for heating and cooking and to power a generator. In the last years he was experimenting with solar with some success."

"Did his housekeeper live on the island, too?"

"Yes." Taylor shrugged. "And I told you yesterday, I don't know anything about their relationship. She was in her mid-thirties when she died and he was ninety or so."

"What was her story?" asked Henry.

"I only met her once or twice. She was a recluse just like Mr. Faraday. Talk among locals is that she arrived in the Keys with a drug problem and he took her in and helped her. She stayed and never went back to family. I don't know if she even had anyone."

"And we're here only because she died," observed Sybil in a wistful voice.

Bert cleared his throat. "So let's learn all we can about this island."

Taylor took that as a cue to continue. "There is a lovely beach on the south end of the island. And you'll find a few coves, quiet little inlets around the perimeter, just big enough for a small vessel to put in. But the only spot to dock is the dock." She chuckled. "The ocean redesigns the island every few years, adding deeper coves or moving them. And the vegetation is thick, especially away from the cottage. You'll find some overgrown paths and the remnants of a garden. We'll tour the cottage, then have lunch on his lovely veranda with a great view back to the mainland. After lunch you all can explore the island, but Josh wants us back to the dock by three-thirty because he has to get ready for the sunset cruise."

She was bombarded with questions just as Josh called, "All of you going ashore, get ready. Taylor can you get yourself on that dock to tie us up?"

"I'll do that," called out the group's sailor. As Josh guided his craft toward the island and close to the pier, Bert leaped onto the aging planks to make the launch fast. Soon everyone was ashore, helping Taylor carry lunch and supplies toward the cottage.

The walk along the almost hidden pathway raised a lot more teasing. Taylor laughed and threatened to make someone walk the plank on the return trip unless they stopped. It was a short, overgrown distance to the Faraday cottage. The first view suggested a comfortable, welcoming home. The roof supported solar panels. The pillars that surrounded the outside of the structure were made of that regional coastal shell and sand mixture making the small home look secure and snug. But Taylor had been correct. The vegetation was moving in. Vines seemed to be reaching out for the pillars and palms were leaning in as though whispering to one another.

The house was designed or had evolved into a great indoor-outdoor living space with rooms that had large windows and doors that opened to the outside. The living area opened to a wide, screened lanai that transitioned to an open patio with an outdoor fireplace and grill.

"I can see why this fellow stayed here," said Kenley. "He had all he needed."

They walked into the kitchen as Sybil exclaimed, "A stove and a microwave! He did have everything he needed."

Henry teased, "Well, sweetheart, he cooked like you. Nuking everything!"

"Now, Henry, you stop. You know I cook dinner once in a while." Everyone laughed. This cousin thing was turning out to be fun.

Casey was very quiet as he checked each room and studied the various doors and windows with his investigator's eye. Taylor walked over to him as he stood staring into Mr. Faraday's bedroom. "Is something wrong?"

"Someone's been here." He looked concerned.

"Yes, the authorities were when they cleaned out Mr. Faraday's things. Then my firm sent us younger attorneys out to clean files and a crew came out to clean out the food and things that would rot. They took clothing and food but left furniture."

"No." He shook his head. "Someone else has been here." He didn't know how to explain his feelings.

"Anyone with a boat could come out. We don't patrol the area." Taylor was uneasy because her husband had expressed a similar suspicion. He had motored out with her last week to help prepare for the cousins' visit.

"Do you mind if I walk around outside?" Casey had a strange feeling - like someone left a negative vibe. Then he laughed at himself. Maybe he was just bored with teaching and wanted to get back into police action.

"Have some lunch then you're free until we leave at three-thirty." Taylor urged him back to the lanai. Once he was moving, she called everyone on the veranda. "Time to eat and talk," she announced. "All of you have to come to terms about this property. There is also some cash. That's what I'm using to cover your travel expenses. Mr. Faraday was an inventor and enjoyed his life here and he continued to develop small items for the refinery industry. About twenty years ago, he negotiated the sale of his patents with a company who then accepted his new ideas for a fee. He told me once, he made the sale because he thought he would be dead soon." She shook her head. "He never expected to live this long, but he had what he needed to be comfortable."

She spread out the luncheon and the cousins helped themselves and settled down for the required discussion. "We have to decide today what we'll do?" asked Kenley.

No," replied Taylor. "My firm wanted you all to see the estate. Remember yesterday in all that paperwork, I explained that we created a partnership and that my firm would act on your behalf to accept offers or solicit ideas, or whatever you all wish. But you don't have to all keep coming here to take action. And nothing will happen until you all agree."

"I read the contract last night," said Bert. "It is pretty simple just protecting us from one of us going in some crazy direction alone and protecting us from any scam artist. It works for me." The others nodded. They had all read the paperwork.

Boz scanned the group. "I'm just delighted to have family." Sybil sniffed at his openness. "Ah, honey, don't cry. This is too nice a day."

Henry put an arm around his wife. "She gets sentimental. You should have seen her when the kids graduated from high school. I don't know what she'll do at a college graduation."

"Oh, Henry!" She swatted at him and the cousins laughed. They continued to speculate on the future of the island. Taylor took notes and promised to get answers to some of their questions.

When the talk seemed to wear down, Casey said, "I'm going to stretch my legs before we report back to Josh."

Boz said, "I think I'd like to take some photos of the house. It might be a great movie location."

"I saw some board games," said Kenley. "Anyone want to try Yahtzee?" Henry and Bert nodded. Taylor and Sybil cleaned up lunch and sat in the lanai to enjoy a quiet afternoon.

Casey walked the perimeter of the overgrown yard and noted three small recently trampled pathways. Leaves had been pushed back or trod upon. The underlying sand gave no clue about a trespasser. He decided to follow each path into the vegetation, looking for evidence of an interloper. At his first choice, he walked along a narrow indentation into the overhanging fronds. It twisted and turned until he found himself at a small clearing. Had someone camped there? The grasses were flattened. He scanned for evidence - nothing. But he felt a prickle at the back of his neck. Was someone watching? Or was he worried about Taylor's Florida lizards crawling on his skin? He laughed at himself. He had to admit he was distracted and apprehensive about coming face to face with some overgrown gecko. But he couldn't shake the feeling of being watched. He stood silently for several minutes. He finally turned back toward the cottage to pick up his next path.

Passing by the cottage he noted that Taylor and Sybil were still lounging in the lanai and he could hear the good-natured chatter from the Yahtzee game. He smiled to himself. He was enjoying his cousins. Thinking over yesterday and today he was lost in thought as he followed the next path. It went directly to a small cove. The vegetation was crushed and broken as though someone had pulled a small craft ashore. How small a boat could safely negotiate these waters? He had no idea. Maybe it wasn't a boat, maybe it was a diver or swimmer who had come ashore, leaving his transport anchored off shore. He squinted out to the ocean, always awed by its vastness. Nothing as far as he could see. It was not like he could spot a parking pole with a sign, *Pay at the Kiosk*. Now he chided himself for being silly.

He was sorry he hadn't thought to scan the horizon from the edges of the island during the morning as they motored in to see if boats were anchored nearby. He'd have to take note on the return to the mainland. See if anything suggested an intruder offshore waiting for them to leave. He made certain he would study the ocean area open to view from the last path.

Stopping along the last path he did as he had on the other two trails, he stood silently for several minutes. This time he heard something. He waited. And was disappointed because the sound was covered as cousins were calling to one another. They must have finished the Yahtzee game and were taking a last look around. He continued down the path and again came to a tiny cove.

As he scanned the horizon he heard a whistle and shouts, Taylor and Josh were calling all hands back to the dock. Just as he turned he noted a footprint hidden under a large fern-like leaf in a damp spot. Taking out his cell he snapped a photo. Stepping around this evidence he walked back to the small cove. More closely inspecting the area, he noted an overhanging palm tree. The base of the palm trunk had been abraded. Had someone tied up in the cove? Recently or sometime in the past? He scanned the area for other hints of an intruder. Nothing. But he wanted to show Taylor.

His thoughts strayed. Taylor. Maybe she would be interested in dinner this evening and listening to his theories. Or maybe she would just be interested in dinner and a Saturday night in the Keys. Something to pursue after he showed his evidence.

Trotting back to dock he heard Sybil moan, "Henry, I left my sunglasses on that table."

"I'll go get them," said her husband.

"And hurry that kid," shouted Josh at Henry's back. Because he was waiting for Boz to appear.

"Taylor?" Casey whispered. "Do we have time for me to show you something?"

Josh heard the request. "You got ten minutes then I take off no matter who's missing. Where is that kid?"

Casey pulled the attorney onto the small pathway. It ran away from the dock along the edge of a mound of dried vegetation curving in a few yards taking them out of sight of Josh's launch and toward the cove and footprint. When they arrived Casey quickly made his case, showing her the print and explaining his theory.

She smiled at him. "You really are a detective." She pushed other fronds aside and found nothing else. "You may be correct, but I don't think this represents anything more than some curious citizens looking around. We didn't find vandalism or anyone's trash on our other visits."

"You think I'm just suspicious by nature?"

"I think you're cautious by training. You're a professional investigator."

He was pleased at her response and thought dinner was looking better and better. The boarding whistle sounded again. "We have to get back." He moved aside to allow her to lead the way. Even in her baggy capris, following her was a treat. The craft came into sight as Josh saw them and waved. He then looked at his watch, scowled as Bert stood ready to cast off the lines. Hopping aboard Josh revved his idling engine.

"He's angry," said Taylor.

Just as she spoke Josh gave one more rev and the small tour boat exploded. Casey pulled Taylor to the ground and rolled into the vegetation. They huddled under the low, large leaves for cover until the debris settled. As quiet returned to the island she pushed his hand away. He had embraced her as they tumbled for cover and had not released her. She whispered, "Thank you for being so protective. My husband will appreciate your efforts." She was close enough, even in the shade, to see him turn red.

"You're married?" he whispered as she tried to get up. "Sorry." He still held her fast as he listened. No calls for help. No splashing. No survivors!

She struggled against his chest. "Someone may need us."

"I don't think there are survivors," he whispered solemnly. "I haven't heard a sound."

"We can go look."

"We're not going out there." He continued holding her under the leaves, reminding himself it was for her safety.

"Let me guess," she whispered, angry, "You think the explosion was no accident and that the lady from Maine was murdered, and the housekeeper, too." He wondered how she could sound so snarky with sand in her mouth.

"Housekeeper?"

"Yes," she sighed, "my husband thinks she was murdered and he thinks it's about this estate." She brushed sand from her face "He's a detective, too."

"I hadn't thought that far," rasped Casey giving the facts a thorough review. He tentatively raised his head and scanned the area. "If he's correct, there's a chance the bomber may still be on the island and looking for us." He lowered his head and lowered his voice so that she almost had to lip read. "Why'd he let you come out here today?"

She turned her head into his chest. "He wasn't happy that I came and he's probably seen the explosion from the mainland. I'm sure he's started out to find me already." She waited a beat. "He was here to investigate the housekeeper's death. And his detective sense whispered to him. Sort of like yours."

"What made him suspicious?"

"He wasn't certain. But when the lady died in Maine after getting my letter, he had several questions about the estate." She tried to get up, but Casey held her down.

"Listen," he whispered.

"To what?" she whispered back.

"I thought I heard branches crack or something. Do you have a gun in your purse?"

She tried to roll her eyes at him. "I always carry one to encourage buyers to close the sale." Snark again?

"Sorry. I just want us to stay safe until help arrives." He froze hearing unfamiliar sounds again.

Taylor caught his wariness. "I'm sure Scott will be here soon. We can scan the waterfront for him."

"We're not moving!" They were silent until Casey asked, "Now I'm the only heir alive, right?" He gave her a worried look. "And if I didn't set the bomb, we're not moving from here to become targets."

She looked very uncomfortable as he made that statement. Her watch pinged. She wiggled her wrist. "The cavalry is closing in." She whispered into the watch face. Read a text reply. "He says stay where we are. He has my signal."

Casey chuckled, "Will he think that I killed everyone because I'm the last heir?"

She squinted at him and asked, "Do all you law enforcement types have that same sick sense of humor?"

"Taylor?" A worried shout filled the lush landscape.

~~~

After several hours of routine investigation, Scott Waterman welcomed Casey into the Waterman residence. The detective was the Key West regulation male; tanned, fit and smiling. "I hate that Taylor has to work on Saturdays. And now this." He threw his arm out. "Have a seat."

Casey looked around a small, aging cottage that seemed to totter on a postage-stamp sized lot. It wasn't Faraday's island cottage, but it did have charm. "This looks comfortable."

"Make yourself at home, I'll get us some beers." Scott took two steps and stood in the center of the kitchen. "I guess we could have moved away but we like the life of the Keys and we wanted to be close to our jobs." He handed a beer to Casey. "So, give me your take. You're one of my eye witnesses."

"Taylor was there, too," Casey reminded him. He thought for a moment. "And I think the killer was there, too."

"Right," nodded Scott, "my guys say this was no accident. The evidence team is combing through the water collecting debris and bodies. As soon as they finish, they'll search the island. It's only been a few months since the housekeeper died. They'll have prior notes and photos for comparison." Gulp of beer. "But I agree, they'll find evidence of a visitor."

Taylor came into the house weighed down with files and a briefcase. "I got everything that goes with Mr. Faraday. He's been a client at the firm for fifty years." She gave that historic note some thought. "We weren't a firm then. But he must have been with one of the original partners who formed and reformed with others until we're us today." She dropped the files on the table and gave Scott a kiss. Casey groaned.

Scott laughed. "She told me you tried a little grab ass."

"I wasn't that crude," Casey defended himself. "But she is beautiful. And I was thinking about asking her to dinner." Taylor gave him a kiss on the cheek.

Scott looked out the window onto the street. "Moss and Cindy are coming here to look over these files. They're bringing dinner." He studied Casey. "I want you to stay here until you leave the Keys."

"Why?"

"Someone's killing heirs and the TV cameras got pictures of you and Taylor."

Casey nodded. "I agree we heirs were the target. So the murderer knows I'm alive. Hmmm." He looked around the small house. "I sleep on that sofa?"

"No," said Scott, "we have a little rental out back. The guy we bought this from made some nice change renting it out." Taylor laughed and Scott scowled at her. "We tried it when we first moved in. But I had to arrest our first renter. He was operating some tourist scam. We just keep it for friends and family now. Moss and his family moved in for a few weeks after the hurricane. I don't know how him, a wife and two kids fit in, but they managed."

Once Moss, Cindy and dinner arrived the team read and reread all of Taylor's files and all of Scott's notes including those from the investigation of the housekeeper's death. It was a long night. Casey finally asked, "Did you have any concerns about Faraday's death?"

"Nah," said Cindy. "He had himself transported to the hospital because he was feeling poorly. It was his heart. He died about three days later. No one was surprised."

Scott ended the work night as he said, "We meet again tomorrow afternoon. Everyone think about scenarios. The team on the island may have more information. Moss, take Casey to pack up his stuff at the hotel. He's staying here."

The other detective grinned, "You mean he's staying in the Moss Family Memorial Shack?"

~~~

Sunshine, sand and ocean, thought Casey as he ran through the Waterman's neighborhood. It was a pleasant early morning run. But he had to chuckle as he ran in his shorts and torn t-shirt, because the folks here thought it was cold in February so they all wore sweatshirts or jackets. He just hoped he got back home before the blizzard arrived that was predicted by The Weather Channel. He trotted into the yard and found Scott glowering from the porch. "I had you stay here to be safe. Not to run around inviting another murder attempt."

"Sorry." Casey wiped his face with his shirt.

"What the fuck?" Scott hopped down the stairs and pulled at Casey's t-shirt. "What's this?" He pointed to scarring on his visitor's chest.

Casey said, "It goes with this." He turned so Scott could see the scarring on his shin. "That's why I had to retire. It's taken more than a year for me to run again."

"That must be some story," suggested Scott. And the story lasted through breakfast.

~~~

After lunch the investigators assembled again. Moss brought the new information gathered from the island. "All the people are accounted for except that Henry guy."

"He's not our killer," said Casey.

"He's the only one not floating in the bay," Cindy challenged his statement. They argued and tried out different theories. No matter how well Casey felt he knew the man, Henry remained the only body unaccounted for. And Scott's prime suspect.

Casey turned to Taylor. "What about the heirs' heirs?" It sounded like a stupid question but she nodded that she understood.

"I've been talking to my boss," she explained. "Since all of you signed the forms yesterday, legally inheriting, everything goes to everyone's estate." They all scowled at her. "I mean that Sybil had children so they inherit her share. I'll have to contact lawyers for the others and see if they had wills and advise them that their clients' estates have grown." She slumped at the table. "I'll never clear up this estate!"

Scott pulled her onto his lap and nuzzled her ear. "Job security. Mortgage payments, babe." His guests booed his mercenary attitude.

Monday morning Scott dropped Casey at the airport. "We'll keep you in the loop, partner. I'm on my way out to the island this morning after I meet with my boss. Watch your back."

"Thanks for the hospitality. And I will be watching my back. There's a blizzard moving in. I can't imagine that our perp will follow me home." Casey grabbed his carry-on and waved to his new friend hoping the blizzard didn't shut down flights until he got home.

~~~

Pending blizzard. Anticipation! That was the attitude around campus. Casey had met with his Tuesday morning class and made certain he had electronic copies of all reports. "I'll have something to do during the snow," he teased the class. He left the early morning class, got to his office and checked his phone. That was when he realized he had left it on airplane mode. Boy, he must have been really tired when he got in last night. Settling at his desk he got his phone back to normal and a message popped up from Scott: *Found Henry's body.*

Casey tried to return the call but it went to voicemail. He left a message, got to his next class, grabbed lunch afterward, and finally settled back at his desk. Tuesday afternoon was set aside for office hours. It was a good opportunity to catch up on work he had ignored during his Florida jaunt. He thought about

Scott's message. All bodies were accounted for. He really was the only heir still alive. Would Scott decide he was the killer? Maybe he should do a little of his own investigating while waiting for Scott to call.

A memory niggled. He had promised Boz Greco to check out his career on Google. Casey smiled sadly. Boz was the first real life actor he had ever met and he had proven to be an entertaining drinking companion. Typing the name into the search bar he watched as several options bubbled to the screen. Photos and various reference sites appeared. Casey squinted at the photos. The actor identified as Boz Greco looked a little different than Casey remembered but he thought actors used make-up and probably airbrushed photos. Boz had said he had a flexible face. He scrolled through the photos of Boz and found one with him standing next to Tom Hanks. Casey clicked on that photo. He studied it, enlarged it. Thought about the small man he had spent a day with. Boz had only reached his arm pit. He was a tiny guy. Casey googled, *How tall is Tom Hanks?* The answer: *Six feet.* He flipped back to the photo of Tom and Boz. Tom was standing next to a man who seemed to be equal in height. Casey was six feet. Hmm. Being retired didn't mean his cop instincts retired. He knew important information when he saw it. He reached for his phone just as it buzzed. It was Scott. He wanted to FaceTime.

"You get my message?" The suntanned detective stared out of the phone.

"Yeah. Did he die in the crash?"

"Nope." Scott frowned. "He was knocked out and pushed into the water too far away from the explosion. We found him in one of those little coves. I don't think he could have been on the launch. Taylor said that's probably why Josh looked angry. He was missing a passenger and was going to leave him behind."

Before Casey could say more Scott barreled on. "We got nothing now. I sent the evidence people back to the island with a fine-toothed comb."

Casey waved into his phone screen. "Listen. That Boz Greco guy was a fake. Can you get prints off the body?" Casey went on to explain his Tom Hanks' theory. They talked and rethought and reformulated theories.

Finally, Scott said, "What's that?" He pointed behind Casey.

"That's snow. We're in for a blizzard. I should get home. I check on a few neighbors."

Scott laughed. "Look out my window." He turned his phone screen to the window. Casey knew what he would see - sunshine, sand and ocean. Scott was gleeful. "You gotta be crazy to live there." Then he got serious. "You're the only heir left. Be careful. I'll start looking for this guy from my end." They ended their conversation with a few more cautions from Scott.

Casey drew two conclusions from the phone call. One, he was the remaining heir to a small island and, two, he was possibly a future murder victim. He glanced out the windows. The clouds were releasing taunting flakes, he could smell the blizzard. It was time to get home. Any murderer would need a snowplow to find him.

As he was packing to go home one of his students, Chris, currently a local police officer working on a criminal justice degree, stopped him. "Casey, did that guy find you?"

"What guy?"

"Some guy that looked Hawaiian or something." Chris was pulling on gloves getting ready to face the weather.

Bells and whistles went off in Casey's head. "How tall?"

"About your height."

The suspicious professor asked, "Could you look at this photo? He called up the photo of Boz Greco and Tom Hanks.

"That's him." Bingo!

"I hope he can find me in the snow." Casey thought a moment as he watched Chris head down the hall. "Chris?" he called. "You have duty tonight?"

"Yeah, I go on at five. Me and Tony are paired in the big SUV tonight. You know that one with the winch?" He was excited to have that duty. Casey thought he wouldn't even notice the cold until about three in the morning.

"Could you guys do a welfare check on me and my neighbors about six or so? I'll check them as soon as I get home." Casey lived on a small lake that was lively all summer but only had five full time winter residents. Except for him the others were elderly. He usually made a point of checking on them before and during bad weather. They had all taken care of him during his year of recovery and rehab from the shooting that ended his career.

"Sure."

"And if you see that guy who asked about me, take him in because he's not used to this kind of weather."

"Sure thing," chuckled Chris. "Some folks think we exaggerate our weather."

Driving home Casey went into security protection mode, planning for his survival. He had a weapon in the car that he moved from its lockbox to a handy pouch on the front of his parka. He made certain his cell phone was in a side pocket. He re-laced his snow boots and slipped on his gloves, the ones that allowed his finger tips to be released. They were the damnedest things, like having little hats for his fingers. But fingers had to be free to use his phone and his gun.

Once he was on the road around the lake, he scanned each house, especially the vacant ones. Randomly he wondered if the summer residents were all wintering in Florida. Shaking the sunshine visions aside, he finally found what he expected. At a vacant house a vehicle had entered the drive disturbing the snow. The driver had left the car close to the house. Casey looked for tracks to see where the driver might have gone. He couldn't see tracks but he suspected someone was out in the darkening snowscape, watching and waiting. Surprised that the perp would come out in this weather, Casey reviewed all the options he had anticipated. Plan B. He would go straight to his snowmobile parked at the side of the house. If he left his SUV parked outside, it would be a hint to Chris that something might be wrong. He hoped the welfare check came on time.

Plan B required that he never enter his house. He liked the idea of being outside with space to run. Parking his SUV in front of the house he scanned the area. It was almost dark and the snow seemed to be falling silently in sheets. He walked to the side of the house and listened.

The grounds around the lake hosted many large trees, providing gifts of shade in the summer, but creating a spooky landscape in winter. Long branches stretched overhead as the snow cloaked them and the ground in white. There weren't patches of brambles, or clusters of saplings, no places to hide along the lake shore. It made running along the trail easier, but made a running victim easier to spot. He heard a crunch. Someone was walking in the trees beside the house. He grasped the cover of the snowmobile and pulled it, walking along the vehicle.

Standing with the tarp in his hands he heard a voice, "Don't move."

"Well, if it isn't the real Boz Greco." He heard a small gasp and, as he turned, continued, "I'm surprised you came in this blizzard."

Greco moved so Casey could see him clearly. "I'm ready for snow. I had a role in *Zero Chill*." He chuckled and indicated his clothing. "This is the kind of gear I used." He was dressed like an Arctic explorer, holding a gun.

Damn, thought Casey, he has finger gloves, too. "So are you planning to be the last heir?"

"Everyone dies and I show up saying that ass Pedro Chen tried to convince everyone he was me and claim the prize. Pretty smart, don't ya think?" He waved the gun. "Move away from your machine."

"What's the plan? I'm committing suicide or something?" Casey inched closer to Boz, still holding the snowmobile tarp.

Boz laughed. "You're making this too easy. Nah, I'm using a scene from one of my other movies." He was very pleased with himself.

"Yeah?" And Casey flung the snowmobile cover at the man knocking him off balance. He was in no mood to listen to Boz brag about his cleverness or his lack of regret killing the cousins. That would come later. When Plan B wrapped up. Casey rushed at him and pushed him, wrapped in the tarp, into the snow and continued running onto the small walking path that circled the lake.

Boz recovered cursing and threatening. Finding his gun in the snow, he finally struggled to his feet. A wind was now scattering snow and making visibility almost non-existent. He shouted, "Asshole, this is snow. I can follow your footprints." He muttered to himself, put his gun in his pocket, and hopped on the snowmobile. He shouted again, "You're making this too easy. You left the keys." Straddling the seat he revved the engine and turned on the headlight. The angle of the lamp made Casey's footprints pop out like big black polka dots in the white snow. Boz took off.

Casey had walked and run this trail throughout his recovery. He knew every inch in every kind of weather. He knew every twist and turn. He raced around a sharp bend and ducked behind a large rock pillar already coated in snow. The pillar was one of the remnants of the days when a grand hotel had attracted vacationers to the lake. The other pillar stood opposite bracketing a smooth path of snow running down to the lakeshore. Plan B, thought Casey as he found the walking stick that he kept at the spot for times he had needed assistance getting back home still leaning against the pillar. It had been months since he had needed help. It was still here waiting like a faithful friend. Before he took his position behind the pillar, he cast snowballs down the path creating false footprints of his downhill direction. Easy-peasy, the evidence suggested that the victim had headed down the path to the shore. He waited. And hoped Boz's greed would make Plan B a success.

The pathway was almost straight as Boz followed the footprints. He increased his speed. The path seemed to run on a gentle incline. More gas to make the climb quicker. More gas for speed. The headlamp jiggled, scattering light off each individual flake. Boz raced trying to keep the footprints in sight and was surprised as the light cut through the sheets of snow outlining a tree or pillar or something that appeared to jump in front of him. He veered to the right and continued on toward the top of a small ridge. Once over the ridge the snowmobile picked up more speed on its downhill run. Unable to adjust for the geography and speed, rider and snowmobile became airborne over the lake.

Casey heard Boz yell as he found no solid ground. So much for Plan B, thought the detective. Running up to the ridge top, really a small hillock at almost lakeside, he scanned the invisible horizon. He watched as the snowmobile headlight and, presumably, its driver bounced on the frozen lake several times like a pebble skipping in the water. The vehicle continued its icy slide toward the center of the small lake. All Casey could see was the headlamp through the thickening flakes. Boz finally appeared to get control of his ride. Tracing a big arc, distinguished by the headlight's movement, he turned the snowmobile back toward the shore. The vehicle flew across the ice, then seemed to shudder.

Casey heard a crack. The ice shouldn't crack. It was too early. But he could see the light swing and jiggle. It tilted, first at a thirty-degree angle which then seemed to spin as though the snowmobile were a bucking bronco up on its hind legs. The snowmobile headlight canted to the sky like some beacon. He was confused; what was the rider doing? Then he heard a scream. The light drew closer to the surface of the ice and soon disappeared.

Casey shouted, "Boz, where are you?" He squinted into the snowy sheets but could not make out any objects on the lake. He called a few more times as he slid on the snow making his way closer to the lake shore.

What the hell? Casey stared into the night. No more noise as the snow settled around him. He puzzled over the problem. Then it hit him. Boz had snagged someone's ice fishing hole. A runner had broken the thin ice that closed a hole and had gotten caught under the surface ice rim. The weight of the engine, the bouncing and sliding, and the motor vibrations may have caused small fissures at the edges of the hole and expanded it to allow the heavy machine and rider to sink into the lake. That wasn't how Plan B was supposed to work. Casey stared into the snow, listening for anything.

"Casey?" An earnest voice called through the blizzard. "Are you out here?"

"Chris?" Casey struggled up toward the path with some effort on the icy ground trying not to slip and roll onto the lake himself. He met the young patrolman along the slippery pathway. They followed the snowmobile tracks, hiking back to the house as Casey explained, "A man missed the path and flew onto the lake with my snowmobile."

"What?" Chris stared into the thick swirling flakes, pointing his flashlight at the lake to find any trace of the accident. "Should I call rescue?"

Casey nodded. "I think we better. Tell them to come in on the low shore. Let's get to your car and meet them." They struggled through the snow back to the patrol car where Tony, the second patrolman, was waiting, standing outside the vehicle, alert, but already covered in snow.

Chris was explaining. "We knew something was wrong. We knew you wouldn't leave your car out on a night like this."

Breathless from trying to keep up with the younger man, Casey huffed, "Yeah, I . . . knew . . . you would . . . catch that." He marveled at how young new recruits were these days.

It turned out to be a long night. No body was found until dawn when the rescue team was able to bring in the appropriate gear for extraction. Casey thought about his plan. It had worked too well. Boz had acted just as he suspected. In Plan B Casey had planned to catch a live perp in some undefined struggle in the snow. Instead, Boz had changed the plan by missing the turn, and ended his quest to be the last heir to Faraday's island.

Did Casey feel guilty? Hell no! Boz was a man who had engineered the deaths of some very fine people. Maybe the last family Casey would ever have.

~~~

As the cold-water divers surfaced and waved, Casey watched the tethered body rise from the icy depths. He took a photo with his phone and sent it to Scott, who immediately called. "Do you know what time it is?"

"Early? And cold!" He slipped his finger back into his glove slot. "We're pulling Boz Greco out of the lake."

"Holy shit! What did you learn?"

"Learn?" Casey was outraged. "He had a gun on me. I distracted him and ran into a blizzard. He stole my snowmobile and followed me. "

"You have a snowmobile?" Murmurs.

"Is that the important question here?"

"Well, I could ask if you're all right." Scott yawned into the phone. "But you woke me up so I guess you're okay."

"He broke the ice and sunk with my snowmobile. One of our rescue teams just recovered his body."

"They dive in ice?"

"We fish in ice, too."

"I guess you closed my case." Murmurs. "Taylor says you have to come visit and tell us all about it."

Casey looked up at the early morning gray sky, thought about sunshine, sand and ocean. "I got spring break in a few weeks."

"We'll save the Moss Family Memorial Shack for you." More murmurs. "Taylor says she's got a friend you should meet."

"Deal."

~~~

Casey arrived at the tiny house on a warm, sunny (What else!) Key West afternoon. Taylor hugged him and said, "I have a friend I want you to meet. She's a maritime researcher." Taylor smiled enthusiastically and Casey had a vision of some sun burnt woman with salt dried skin - probably skinny and old. "She'll be here for dinner."

"Great!" Scott called from the kitchen. "We need time for just us to clear up some loose ends."

"What loose ends?" Casey was still standing in the doorway holding his carry-on bag.

"Give him a chance to shake off the ice. It's been cold in Minnesota." Taylor slipped off her shoes and curled up on the couch ready to listen. Curiosity outweighed her concern for making Casey too comfortable before he told the full story.

Casey dropped his bag and sat beside her while Scott flopped in his easy chair as he announced, "I got information from the guys in California. They found emails between Greco and the little guy, Pedro, talking about changing places. And credit card charges that show Greco was in Maine when the librarian died."

"Pedro wasn't a part of this, was he?" Casey had liked the smiling actor with the flexible face.

"In the emails Greco said he was in rehab and didn't want to lose the inheritance. He convinced Pedro to impersonate him."

"Rehab?" asked Taylor and Casey together.

"Yeah," nodded Scott. "His career was in a tailspin because of drugs and alcohol. He needed money." The detective shook his head. "I don't think Pedro expected to die."

"I want to hear about your snowmobile," said Taylor. And Casey related the story of the blizzard, Plan B and the drowning.

"I guess we've closed this case," Scott summed up.

"What about the housekeeper?"

Scott shrugged. "Greco didn't start planning to eliminate heirs until he got Taylor's letter. I think the housekeeper did just have an accident."

A knock at the door. Taylor jumped up. "That's our guest." She pulled Casey to his feet and dragged him to the door. She didn't notice his wariness. In his opinion no one could be as beautiful as Taylor. "This is Dr. Lydia Herschel," said his hostess. "We call her Hershey because she's so sweet."

And I call her gorgeous, thought Casey as he reached out to shake hands with a slender woman about his age. She had sun kissed skin and dark hair.

"I've been so anxious to meet the owner of that marvelous island," said Dr. Herschel. Scott walked from the kitchen with beers. Hershey and Casey each took one. Scott waved everyone to get comfortable as he sprawled across his big easy chair. "You just got here in time Hershey to hear about Casey and my wife alone in the jungle."

"He said he was protecting me," said Taylor with a teasing sparkle in her eye. "He assured me it was for my safety."

Scott guffawed. "What else did he do?"

"The only reason I hit on your wife was she wasn't wearing a wedding band." It was a lame excuse, and Casey admitted to himself that he had been interested in getting to know her.

She wiggled her fingers at him. "My fingers have been swollen."

"Are you sick or something?" Casey panicked, the girl of his dreams was sick!

"Or something," crowed Scott. "My little mama-to-be."

Casey grinned in relief as he looked around the limited cottage space. "When does this place go on the market? Because there's no room for a baby here."

"We're buying my parent's place near an elementary school. There are advantages to being a Conch." Scott had bragged since meeting Casey about life as a native born Key West favorite son. "We're going to rent this place. We can rent it for more than the mortgage payment." Scott wiggled his eyebrows. "It'll be our college fund. Want a lease?"

"Maybe." His friends gasped. Casey went on to explain. "I'm finishing my teaching obligations at the end of the semester and taking a job with a firm that provides security consulting and offers training to law enforcement. I'll go to regional and national meetings to give seminars or go to local departments and help with training. So I can live anywhere."

"Even your island?" Hershey asked. She had been quietly observing her 'date.'

"I'll stay in Minnesota because of Pop." Casey had talked with his friends at length about his father's health condition. "But I can see coming here whenever there's a blizzard forecast."

"To stay on your island?" Dr. Herschel had a one-track mind.

He turned to the researcher, or as he thought of her, another great reason to keep visiting all this sunshine and sand. He winked at Taylor because she had been doing some research for him.

"Some folks might like to know about donating land to the state university system for research and things," Taylor explained as she waved vaguely to include 'research and things' in her arms.

"Who would want to know that?" asked her helpful husband.

Taylor sat close to Scott on his big chair and cleared her throat. "At the request of my clients," she cut a glance to Casey, "I've spoken with the University and they have access to a state fund to buy properties for research and preservation."

"And who are those clients?" Scott continued his helpful prompts.

She said, "The Ross's two kids and Casey." She wiggled her ringless fingers. "And Taggert's attorney. Kenley Taggert had a will and his real estate will be gifted to New Mexico conservation agencies. I talked with his attorney who says he would agree to conservation of the Faraday estate because it follows Kenley's wishes for his own land." She grinned at everyone. "He also said that he'd turn Kenley's share of the island purchase money back to the project for stewardship of the property." She frowned. "He said it would help with taxes for Kenley's estate as they give out bequests."

Casey grimaced. "The Ross kids and I need our share of the money. It will really help me with Pop's expenses." He thought about the lively people he had met that day whose deaths had created this opportunity for him.

Hershey looked confused. "Does the killer get money, too?"

"The real Greco never signed anything and because he murdered to inherit the estate our laws prohibit him or his estate from gaining from his actions."

"That just leaves Bert O'Keefe." Casey was keeping track of his lost cousins.

Taylor groaned. "That's a whole 'nother story. He is recently divorced from wife three, but never changed his will so she gets everything. And she wants everything. I think she has a notion to hold out for some big development sale." Here the attorney chortled. "Remember all the papers you people signed?"

Casey nodded. "Something about a partnership?"

"My boss has had experience with these multi-heir messes. He suggested the partnership to stop hold-outs from delaying settlements." She was proud of herself. "I set it up as he suggested. After contacting the New Mexico attorney and the Ross kids, I filed papers with you," she grinned at Casey, "as the president and person who makes the final decisions and signs everything."

"Where do I sign?"

The maritime researcher squealed just like some teenage girl coming face to face with her pop singing idol. Sunshine, sand, ocean and new friends.

9. M is for Mystery

Barthélemy Banks

By his count, Tim Malloy had more people try to kill him than he'd ever killed. You'd think it would be the other way round for a professional assassin. He must have really pissed a lot of people off during his years with the CIA.

They say you never retire from the Company, but in Malloy's case they had retired him. Put him out to pasture. Guess you become less useful as a shooter when your hand trembles from too much booze. After his wife had left him for his spotter, he had taken to steady drinking.

That's how he'd wound up here in Key West. As the T-shirts say, KEY WEST IS A DRINKING TOWN WITH A FISHING PROBLEM.

Most days he hung out at Jimmy Buffett's Margaritaville, nursing a frozen drink with a salty rim. He'd never lost the shaker of salt. That's what you do when you're retired, you sit there and wait, although you're not sure for what. For your wife to come back? That wasn't going to happen, and if it did that ship had sailed. For the Company to reinstate him? Wasn't going to happen either.

Every now and again, someone stopped by to kill him. Old enemies. Old targets. Old comrades. So far, nobody had succeeded.

You didn't get to be a top shooter without some better-than-average skills. And he used to be at the top of the game, before he took up booze as a lifestyle.

Thankfully, he was drinking less these days. And as a result his hands shook less.

Today, he was trying a frozen peach margarita. Not bad. Maybe those Georgia peach farmers had something going.

The bartender – a young barista with a ponytail and short shorts – had just delivered a second. He barely noticed the guy who sat on the stool beside him. But his attention snapped into focus when his neighbor muttered, "Hello, M."

M had been his cryptonym with the Company.

"What letter of the alphabet do I call you?" said Malloy as he sipped his new drink.

"You can call me P."

"For Peckerhead?"

"Now don't be that way. I'm being friendly. Don't even have a gun on me."

That was probably a lie, but Malloy didn't challenge him. "So why are you dropping by for a drink? This is not a performance review. I haven't performed in quite a while."

"Got a favor to ask. Direct from B."

"The Big Man?"

"Himself."

"What's this favor?"

"We've got a former KGB man – an old-timer named Nicolas Patishovich. He's willing to talk. About something very important to us. But he doesn't trust us. Says he'll only talk with you."

"Me. I don't know him. But I do know who he is. A shooter, like me."

"That's why he'll talk with you. The two of you were opposite numbers. He's heard of you, too. Says he respects who you were, that he will only talk with you."

"You don't say?"

"We brought him down here. Got him stashed at La Concha Hotel. Need you to step over there with me and see what Patishovich has to say. You'd be doing the Big Man a big favor."

"What's in it for me?"

"Money. I'm authorized to pay you up to a hundred grand. You can buy a lot of margaritas for a hundred grand."

"Okay, I'll do it. But I want to have my desert before we go."

"Sure, eat up."

Malloy ordered a piece of key lime pie, an excuse to palm the fork.

Malloy's Spidey sense told him something was wrong. Had he picked up a foreign accent in P's speech pattern?

"Where you from, P?" Malloy casually asked as he finished his pie.

"Kansas City."

"Me, I'm originally from Wyoming," Malloy said as they left Margaritaville, heading left on Duval toward the hotel.

"Wyomink," said P. "I've never been there."

He'd slightly mispronounced the state.

Malloy remember a course he'd had many years ago at the Monterey Language School. It was a guide to help identify when you are listening to someone speaking English with a Russian accent.

-if they speak in a monotone.
-if they avoid using "to be."
-if they omit little words like "the, a, an, to."
-if they roll their R's.
-if they pronounce a guttural H.
-if they pronounce 'w' as 'v.'
-if they pronounce 'th' as 'z.'
-if they pronounce 'I' as "ee."
-emphasizing the end of "-ing" even turning it into a "k" sound.

Something about P's way of talking was a little off. He'd pronounced "Wyoming" with a "k."

There was one other test he'd learned to rely on, a Russian's difficulty in saying the word "cat." The "a" in "cat" is a front open vowel sound that doesn't exist in Russian, so it's usually substituted with the "eh" sound as in "red." This substitution happens when you don't open your mouth enough and keep the tongue arch high in the mouth.

"Look over there," Malloy pointed. "A cat sleeping in the sun. Do you like cats?"

P glanced at the sleeping feline that Malloy was nodding toward. "Yes, I like cats," he said without thinking. But he pronounced it more like "kets."

Hmm.

~~~

The took the hotel elevator to the 4th floor, walked down the carpeted hallway to Room 410, and stepped inside. A bulky man with a square jaw was sitting on the edge of the bed.

"M, I want you to meet Nicolas Patishovich, the former KGB shooter."

As Patishovich started to stand, Malloy reached forward and stabbed him in the throat with the fork. Blood spurted everywhere. The man made a gurgling sound, reached for his neck, dropping the MP-443 Grach he'd been drawing from beneath his loose tropical shirt.

"What the –?" growled P.

Malloy scooped up the Grach and pointed its squarish barrel toward the phony CIA field agent. "Don't reach for that PYa in the small of your back. This 9×19mm 7N21 cartridge will punch a hole through your skull like a breadknife through warm bread."

"Wait, wait," the man said, raising his arms so his hands were visible. In his excitement, it pronounced the words "Vait, vait."

"You need another thirty days in that Moscow Language School," Malloy said.

"Is that what gave me away? I told them I wasn't ready."

"I wasn't totally sure, but I figured it was safer to kill you either way. Didn't want to deal with the CIA. Didn't want to deal with the Federal Security Service of the Russian Federation. FSB, that's what the KGB is called these days – right?"

"You're going to kill me?"

"Unless you tell me what this is all about. I'm a has-been. Haven't been active in years. What would you want with me?"

"We wanted to turn you," the man said, his voice relaxing to his normal accent. Pronouncing the "w's" as "v's." "Our research suggested you'd be vulnerable, being a drunk." The "v" became a "w." He shrugged, "But I guess we were wrong."

"Looks like it."

Mallory shot him in the forehead.

Then he hurried back to Margaritaville. He needed a drink.

10. That's All She Wrote

Jonathan Woods

We were barrel-assing down Route 1 from Miami to Key West in Ray's rusty old RAM during the tail end of a tropical depression. Windows rolled down because Ray can't breathe in air conditioning. Rain whipping inward. Storm wind howling through the interior like a demon lover, clinking together empty beer cans on the crew cab floor. KLINK, KLANK. KLINK. Candy wrappers, Cheez-It bags with nothing left but cheese dust and a few leftover grains of blow from a wild night swirled in the cab. Jesus, mounted on the dashboard by the truck's previous owner, swayed back and forth in a quasi-religious version of the Texas two-step. Soon enough the storm passed. The semi-tropical sun reappeared, beating down like a ballpeen hammer on a tin roof on the set of a long-lost Tennessee Williams play.

My name's Jimbo.

We passed two dead iguanas on the shoulder and the bloated carcass of a feral hog. Tough luck for the local critters. When had feral hogs made it down to the keys? Damn hogs were taking over the planet.

Just over the bridge southbound to Fiesta Key a steaming single car wreck came up on the right. It looked like the Mustang

119

had shot over the bridge way too fast, clipped the side of the bridge's steel barrier wall and done a double flip before coming to rest in the sea shallows below a poorly banked downward curve. It must have just happened. A man sat stone still in the driver's seat. His door gaped wide open; his head thrust back at an odd, unhuman angle. As Ray slowed the truck, a svelte blonde woman climbed over the probably dead guy and eased her feet down into the shallow sea water. She wore pink panties. Nada más.

She staggered around in the warm, knee-deep water as if she was lost. Or had mislaid her life. Blood streaked her jaunty boobs.

Ray stopped the truck to get a better look, wheels crunching on the gravel verge.

"Hey," I said. "Maybe we should offer a Good Samaritan hand to the maimed and mutilated."

"At least he died getting a blow job," said Ray.

I wasn't convinced that made a difference.

"A risky business when you're going too fast down an unfamiliar two-lane highway and the windshield's fogged up due to lust," said Ray philosophically.

Ray set the parking brake, disembarked and edged down the embankment and right up to the woman, who stood stock still watching him come. When he arrived, she hurled herself against him, wrapping her arms around him in a desperate hug, as if he was about to head off to certain death in Somalia fighting jihadists. I saw her whisper something in his ear. What had she said to him? I imagined what her bare white breasts felt like pressing again Ray's chest. His hands gripped the twin orbs of her buttocks as though they were a god send. Some guys had all the luck.

After a longish, languorous minute, they unfurled. Ray stepped over to the Mustang wreck and put two fingers against the man's neck. Then looked back up at me and shook his head.

I heard her say: "My bag."

Ray ducked down and leaned into the wreck, almost as if he was embracing the dead guy. Reappeared with a canvas tote bag in hand big enough to hold a half dozen dead possums after an all-night possum hunt. When I was growing up in the East Texas piney woods, nothing beat a slow cooked possum stew.

Ray handed the woman the bag, swooped her up in his arms and carried her like a bride up the graded slope, careful about each step he took. Suddenly remembering she was topless, she held one arm across her breasts, the other hooked around Ray's neck.

I was like: Whoa! What's up, dude.

Ray opened the crew cab door and set the woman carefully on the bench seat as if she was made out of something that might break easily.

"There's a T-shirt you can put on in one of those bags on the floor," said Ray.

He winked at me.

"Jimbo, this here is Debbie from somewhere. By some miracle she's virtually unscathed. All that blood belongs to the dead guy. Debbie, this is my best buddy, Jimbo."

She found a white T-shirt and slipped it over her head. It fit pretty good, her nipples hauntingly pert against the thin cotton, like the twin knobs of an old-timey radio. I had this intense desire to change the station, adjust the volume.

Ray cranked the RAM awake and put her in gear.

"Debbie doesn't want to stick around and get caught up in a whole big accident clusterfuck with Highway Patrol and ambulance guys and what not. Doesn't know who the dead guy is. Thought we could give her a lift to Key West."

With a spray of gravel, we sped back onto the roadway.

Well, I thought, this could be interesting. Or weird as shit.

~~~

Why, you may ask, were we barrel-assing to Key West?

Ray is a minor American novelist. Teaches Rhetoric and Communication Skills at Key West Community College. I make wedding videos. Key West is a big wedding destination. We'd been hanging out, getting in trouble for years. We'd been up in Miami on a bender. Last stop had been the John Wilkes Booth Tap.

We didn't go there very often because of its Republic ambiance. They even had a photo of a Klan gathering hanging above one of the urinals in the men's shitter. There is no women's pissoir at the John Wilkes Booth Tap. If you were of the female persuasion and had to go, you peed outside between the parked cars in the crushed-seashell-paved parking lot.

We found seats at the bar next to two women with hairy arm pits. The chit-chat was ecumenical as the ladies were of a religious disposition. Both were pretty (but not spectacular) and possessed of outstanding chests and delicate earlobes. Turned out they were both grad students at a small Catholic university and were pining for an academic discussion over a Bombay Martini with a pickled onion (A/K/A a Gibson). Baudelaire. Katherine Mansfield. Sylvia Plath. As the evening wore on, the conversation naturally shifted to out-of-body sex research. Soon enough we (a foursome) where back at our hotel.

[Cut to BLACK]

An urgent rapping on the door of our shared hotel room late the next morning jolted us from a tangle of female flesh.

"Door's open," said Ray, pulling on his road-worn khaki shorts.

Giggling, the two libidinous Catholic girls drew the sheets of the king bed up to their chins with me between them. A fortyish hotel bellboy in a retro bellboy's cap stuck his head around the door, gave Ray the stink eye, handed him a FedEx envelope.

"Fuck you too, Harry," said Ray, as the aging bellboy departed. How did he know the bellboy's name was Harry?

Ray tore open the FedEx envelope, wrangled out a sheet of pale blue stationary and sailed the envelope across the room in my direction. Being an ex-high-school-hoop-star, I grabbed the FedEx envelop out of the air. Ray gave the letter a look of worried puzzlement.

"Well, shit," he said.

He crushed the stationary into a ball and crammed it into a pocket. The scent of el cheapo cologne (on clearance at Marshall's) wafted from the crushed paper, crossed the room and whacked my sinuses like nettles. The return address on the FedEx envelope read: Wanda Smith care of Ray's Victorian house in Key West. A couple of years ago Ray had inherited the house from a childless rich uncle in the roadside furniture store business. Along with the house came a classic, fully-restored, yellow Stingray (like the one Joan Didion drove) and several paintings which Ray asserted were of great value—including one of Ulysses S. Grant taking a piss at the side of the road in the summer of 1864. Ray's uncle had been found in the trunk of his Coup de Ville with a bullet hole in the back of his head.

"Come on, Jimbo, move your ass," said Ray. "We've got to get back to Key West ASAP."

"Bad news?"

"Good guess," said Ray.

He drew a black T-shirt over his ultra-hairy chest, shoved his cellphone in his back pocket, checked for his wallet and keys. I leaped up and was ready to go in five. We dashed out the door and down the hall toward the elevator, leaving the two buck naked Catholic girls to their own devices.

Since Ray often travelled on "business," from time to time he allowed a femme fatale to reside rent free in the Key West house. To keep the place tidy and shipshape. To make sure vagrants didn't break in and take up residence. The latest, heavily tattooed and calling herself Wanda Smith, had even managed to finagle herself partway into Ray's heart.

As we climbed into Ray's truck brought around by a valet guy, I asked:

"Wanda?"

Ray nodded. His eyes said, soon to be dead Wanda.

~~~

Now halfway to Key West, Ray and I and Debbie proceeded apace down ye olde Route 1. After an appropriate period of mourning for the dead guy, Debbie leaned over into the front seat. The pong of recent wild sex intoxicated. Her blond hair, chin length, swayed in the AC. A coy nose sniffed. Kissable lips, the kind you linger over, offered themselves in flamboyant vagina pink lip-gloss, slightly parted to display dazzling pearly whites cast in a carnal grin. Almond-shaped eyes the color of stone-washed blue jeans gazed at me, then Ray. In summary: lush, cocky and fearless.

"Thanks for stopping, guys," she said. "That was a bit of a tight squeeze."

"Hey, no problem," said Ray. "Want something to drink."

"Got any Jack?"

"Sorry, sweetheart, we're shit outa Jack. But we've got half a paper cup of cold coffee with two sugars and a spritz of Half & Half. Or a diet Coke with all the ice melted."

She turned and looked at me.

"You there," she said. "Maybe you'd like to help a girl out?"

"Hey, I'm a good listener."

"What kind of cock you got hangin' there between your legs? I mean, is it dying for some action? 'Cause I wanted to suggest maybe stopping at a motel. Of course you'd get the two for one rate."

"Oh, man, I'd love to," said Ray. "But I'm being treated for a sexually transmitted disease."

Yeah, right, I thought.

Ignoring Ray, Debbie ruffled her hand through my hair.

"You on board with a little X-rated divertissement, sport?"

I looked at Ray.

"Hey, Bat Man," I said. "How about we stop at a gas station so Debbie and I can use the men's room. You can get some cigarettes. Ice cold drinks. Fill the tank."

"Sorry, no can do, Robin. Key West is calling me el pronto."

"Oh, baby," lamented Debbie.

She reached for Ray's crotch, but he batted her hand away.

"Who was the dead guy?" asked Ray.

"Don't start with that shit," said Debbie. "I was just workin'. He picked me up outside the Miami bus station where I'd just arrived on an all-night bus from Birmingham."

"What the heck were you doing on an all-night bus from Birmingham?"

"I had to leave Birmingham quick like a bunny 'cause the asshole I was living with robbed a high stakes poker game and every mobster in town was looking for him and his associate, me. Story of my life. Anyway, I was just standing there outside the bus station, taking in the Miami skyline, minding my own business, when this car stops. The front passenger window rolls

126

down. Single guy behind the wheel says, 'get in.' I lean down and look at him. He's wearing shades, a white shirt and tie, gray slacks. And his dick's stickin' out of his fly like the fucking leaning tower of Pisa. And since I had a cash flow problem, I said to myself: 'What the hey?'"

"Swell. So you were a Birmingham debutant?" asked Ray.

She laughed. It was a dark, haunted laugh.

"Nah. I pretty much move with the wind. Before Birmingham, I lived out in west Texas. Worked the oil fields for a while."

"Is that right?"

"Hold up, now. How'd we get so far off topic? Enough about me. How's your dick hangin', cowboy. Limp? Or the opposite? It's a shame you won't let me help you out in that department."

"It's Ray, sweetheart," said Ray. "Not cowboy. And the status of my dick is private."

With a sigh Debbie sat back.

"You're bummin' me out," she said. "I'm totally broke. Should have taken that dead creep's wallet."

We drove on in silence for a while. Then I tapped Ray on the shoulder and pointed to the gas gage which had slipped into the "hey, douchebag, you're in the zero, zip, zilch, nada zone." Just then we were coming into Marathon Key, one of the more populous keys. We passed several bars, a gym, a secondhand furniture store, a CVS, a vape and CBD oil shop, a tattoo parlor and a liquor store. At the liquor store Debbie said:

"Well, gents, since y'all don't seem to be the least bit interested in my twofer offer, just let me out here."

"You sure?" asked Ray.

"How the fuck is it your business whether or not I'm sure?" she snapped.

Ray stopped the truck. Debbie dismounted.

"Good luck," I said, leaning out the window to take in her glorious stats one last time. Ray's white T-shirt was long enough to more or less cover Debbie's pink-pantied privates. I noticed she had a couple of tats on her legs. Tropical themed. (I have a love hate relationship with tats on chicks. Oddly erotic on the one hand. Ugly-as-fuck graffiti on the other.) Her skin was golden. She'd rolled up the sleeves of the T-shirt to show her river-stone-smooth rounded shoulders. Was I in love or in lust? Did it matter?

With a puff of air, she flipped me the bird and pushed through the glass door of the liquor store.

We continued down the main drag to an Exxon station and filled her up.

"Man, I could eat something," said Ray.

"Me too."

By chance the gas station doubled as a fried fish takeout joint. We ordered shrimp baskets and Mexican Coca-Colas and a side of onion rings. At the edge of the gas station lot, we pulled over and ate like jackals. Done, Ray wiped his fingers with a moist towelette.

"Damn that was good. But we've got to get going," said Ray.

He turned the ignition key. The engine rumbled alive. He reached out and adjusted his side mirror.

"Oh, shit."

I looked behind.

Running toward us, barefoot, purse over one shoulder, boobs bouncing like wildebeests on the run, waving frantically, it was Debbie. My nether regions stirred.

Ray's RAM waited. She caught up, opened the crew cab door and jumped in.

"Whew."

"I guess Marathon sucked eggs," said Ray.

"If I were you," said Debbie. "I'd step on it."

In one hand she held a snub-nosed .38 Special. In the other her canvas bag yawned open, revealing a goodly clump of cash.

"Thought you said you were broke," said Ray.

"Was," she replied. "That liquor store was an f-ing windfall. But we should blow town before the owner breaks out of the closet I locked him in."

She grinned, happy as a lark at her newfound liquidity.

At a stoplight Ray held his phone left-handed down between his legs and texted me: "Nd 2 dmp ths honey asap."

As we rumbled out of Marathon headed southward again, Debbie pulled a pint of Jack from her bag, twisted off the cap and took a long swig before passing it to me. What choice did I have? I too took a long swig. Passed the bottle to Ray. Etc. Etc.

Dropping the empty bottle on the floor, Debbie climbed over the seatback into the front seat. Be still, my heart. She had taken off her panties but not the T-shirt.

"This one's gratis. Which is French for *on the house*, baby. Just in case you don't speak French."

Through the thin cotton, I kissed her nipples as if they were wild strawberries. My penis morphed into a Mayan stone dildo upon which Debbie forthwith impaled herself. Oh, God! Afterward, she disimpaled herself. Looked over at Ray, whose eyes had never left the highway.

"Hey, stud. Lighten up. You're next. After I pee."

"Pee?"

"Yeah, pee. My bladder overfloweth."

Moments later Ray pulled onto the shoulder and stopped. Thick mangroves snarled from both sides of the highway.

"You're such a gentleman," said Debbie. "Be right back."

She opened the crew cab door, jumped down and over a narrow ditch, her bag slung over her shoulder. Partially hidden by a clump of cactus, she squatted.

Ray hit the gas.

~~~

A while later (sans Debbie) we passed through Big Pine Key, where the endangered miniature key deer live. Every year a few of them get mowed down by murderous tourists in big, fast cars in a rush to make it to Key West. Especially at night—deer in the headlights as they say. For a brief moment I grew maudlin thinking about those tiny, mangled deer carcasses, their lives cut short by out-of-town assholes with Hemingway fixations.

Around 4:00 p.m. we rolled into the suburb of Stock Island and then Key West. We drove down Truman Street (named after olde Harry S., who'd spent his presidential winter getaways in

Key West) into historic Old Town, turned up a side street and stopped in front of Ray's abode. A Victorian fantasy is the way Ray described his inherited house. Broad porches up and down done up with decorative arches and fancy wicker furniture. The façade a whimsical mishmash of gewgaws and doodads, fish scales and barley twists, painted white with red and yellow trim. Like something out of a Flannery O'Connor story.

"What the fuck!" said Ray, reacting to the absence of the Stingray from the side porte cochère where he always kept it parked.

That was just the beginning.

The paintings (of some considerable value according to Ray). Gone. The rare wines and cognacs. Gone. The finer Art Deco furniture pieces, including the piano, the Persian carpets, the Louis XIV china, the silver. All gone.

"Noooooo!"

Ray's eyes went into orbit. He swooned, collapsing onto the beautiful hardwood floor.

"Shit. Piss. Fuck. Cunt. Twat. Anus. Dick. Clit. Cock. Gook. Jizz. Slut. Penis. Vulva."

Wanda had cleaned him out. Wanda the heart throb had morphed into Wanda the carnivorous grifter in the Grand Guignol tradition.

Ray staggered to his feet and sat on the only piece of furniture remaining in the living room, a cheap leather hassock from India. Somewhere I scrounged up a bottle of small-still bourbon that had been overlooked and poured two glasses. Two cheap plastic beach glasses. I handed one to Ray.

The ultimate insult: On the kitchen counter wrapped in last Thursday's *Key West Citizen*, Wanda had left a whole dead Mangrove Snapper long past its prime. I tossed it out the back door before Ray saw it. The local feral cats would throw one heck of a party later tonight.

"Well, son of a bitch," said Ray, sipping his second bourbon.

He reached into his pocket, pulled out Wanda's crumpled letter on blue linen paper and spread it open.

"Dear Ray," he read aloud. "Fuck you."

'OK," I said. "What else did she say?"

"That's all she wrote," said Ray.

He crushed the letter back into a ball and threw it across the room. It bounced off the wall and lay still. Exhausted, we drank the rest of the bourbon, smoked a jay and crashed.

~~~

The sun woke me about 8:00 a.m., streaming into the uncurtained upstairs bedroom where I'd succumbed to slumber.

Where was I? Oh, yeah, Key West. Why was I here? I'd come to help my friend Ray who's hot patootie Wanda had shown her true colors. Ripped him off down to the studs. I guess he'd really pissed her off somehow. This was her revenge.

When I looked out the bedroom window, Ray's truck was gone. So was Ray.

I called my old girlfriend (Babs). She picked me up and dropped me back at my houseboat on Garrison Bight. I asked her on board for a drink and she stayed the night. Was she hoping to convince me of her long-haul amatory skills?

Ray was absent without leave from his professorial job. After a month the college fired him. Babs and I moved in together. I liked to cuddle. So did Babs. She also liked to fuck.

Two years went by.

Babs and I were still together.

Ray never did return to teaching at Key West Community College. And he sold his dead uncle's Key West house. Wanda's betrayal had ruined it for him.

Over the years I followed in the newspapers Ray's meteoric literary rise. His second novel clawed its way to the top of the *New York Times* best seller list. He got a movie deal. Lived in London, Bogota, Istanbul and wrote political pieces for *The New Republic*.

For our second anniversary of cohabitational bliss, Babs and I flew to Paris for a week in February. She'd always wanted to go there. Check out the Mona Lisa's smile in person. The day we arrived icy winds skated down the Seine. It was colder than a witch's tit.

After checking into lodgings in the Latin Quarter at 9 rue Gît-le-Cœur—formerly the Beat Hotel where Burroughs and Ginsberg had lived back in the 1950's—we sought shelter from the winter blast in a nearby bistro.

There, unbelievably, at the marble-topped bar, drink in hand, wearing an expensive sheepskin coat and a blue wool beret, stood Ray.

And next to him? Who else but Debbie. (You remember her, right?)

Rumors of them hooking up had appeared on the literary gossip sites. And I'd read they were living in Paris. But still, running into them like this was one far-fucking-out fluke.

Six months after our wild ride down to Key West, I'd also come across a story about a woman who'd been found dead in the driver's seat of a yellow Stingray at the bottom of a Louisiana bayou. She'd been there a couple of months (or longer) when they dredged her out. A driver's license found on the body identified the deceased as Wanda Smith. Some said an accident, some suggested suicide, still others voted for foul play—but as far as I know, nothing came of it. What do you think?

As Babs and I walked toward the bar, Ray looked up and recognized me. His eyes flashed delight.

"Well Goddamn, if it isn't Jimbo!"

After a grappling, wrestler-like bro hug, Ray stood back, his arm around Debbie's waist.

"You remember Debbie," he said.

How could I forget? Her braless boobs googling wantonly beneath a gauzy blouse carried me back to the first time we'd met on the road to Key West. Then it had been summertime. Today her nipples stood at attention; she looked chilly.

I smiled. The tip of my dick tingled.

As I leaned over to kiss her on both cheeks in the French style, she whispered in my ear: "How's it hangin', Jimbo?"

Was that the same question she'd whispered to Ray back when he'd rescued her stark naked from the car wreck on Fiesta

Key? That's a conundrum I'll probably never get answered, I thought, as the glorious first sip of a French Pinot Noir exploded on my taste buds. Babs gave me her equally glorious smile and squeezed my hand. Ray was recounting in riotous detail an undertaking with some very bad people he'd been involved with in Morocco, an undertaking that skated on the razor's edge of illegality. As I listened, it occurred to me Ray might very well end up in the trunk of a luxury car, just like his favorite uncle. Or shot dead on a Paris street like Jean-Paul Belmondo in *Breathless*.

But who can predict the kinky and outré twists and turns of fortune? Certainly not me. I'm just along for the ride.

Bonus
An East Job

John Hemingway

Dimitri was sitting in the room above the garage where he worked. He had finished for the day and he was getting dressed to go out. He didn't know exactly where he would go but he figured that it would either be to the Clevelander in South Beach or Bulla in Coral Gables. He was in a mood for cocktails and conversation and was hoping that he might run into the girl who he'd met the other night at the Clevelander. Just the same, it was a long shot. She was quite attractive and hot women like her didn't stay in one place for long. They tended to play the field and he couldn't blame her. When you had it, and she had it in spades, you might as well flaunt it.

He himself didn't have much to flaunt physically. He was medium height, five foot nine, with high cheekbones and light skin that freckled in the summer sun. His eyes were an intense blue-grey and his eyebrows were wild and bushy. His forearms were strong and his hands were calloused after many years working as a mechanic.

He was a romantic man, or at least he liked to think he was. The kind of guy who would do just about anything for a woman. Bring her flowers, write her poetry, fix her car for free, there seemed to be no end to Dimitri's generosity. His only problem was that while he loved women, pretty much all women, they tended to take advantage of his generous character. Rarely would one of them fall in love with him. In fact, he couldn't think of the last time when that had happened. As a result, whenever a woman did find him acceptable and went to bed with him he made the most of it. He did his best to make it a memorable occasion so that the next day she could tell her girlfriends "you know the guy I slept with last night is as ugly as fuck, but he sure knows how to use what little he has."

In short, nothing had ever been given to Dimitri. There were no free lunches, no free rides. Whatever belonged to him he'd had to work for. Indeed, he barely made it out of high school in Moscow. Academics had never been his forté, and even moving to the States had been difficult. The female doctor that had been assigned to him by the US Embassy for his immigrant medical examination came close to failing him due to his high blood/sugar level and his incipient halitosis. Fortunately for Vasily, the embassy didn't pay her much and he managed to change her mind with a $500 bribe and an invitation to dinner at a fancy restaurant downtown. There the two of them dined on roast duck with buckwheat and blinis served with caviar and sour cream. The M.D. considered herself something of an expert when it came to wines and so he ordered an expensive bottle of Amarone from Italy. All together they had three bottles of Amarone and when the wine was gone he asked the waiter to bring them a bottle of vodka for good measure.

Outside the restaurant he suggested that they go to his place but she insisted that he take her home. So he called an Uber and when it stopped in front of her building she was so drunk that he had to carry her up four flights of stairs to her apartment.

Hard physical work he reminded himself just before she fell asleep in his arms. It had always saved the day for Dimitri when it came to women. Not luck. Luck had never been a friend of his.

Recently, however, things had been looking up for Vasily work wise. In Miami he had found a job that paid exceptionally well, ten thousand dollars a night. Not every night, of course, just once a week, more or less. An Italian who said his name was Gino Pavese had heard about Dimitri through a mutual friend and had asked him if he'd like to earn ten thousand dollars a night.

"Who wouldn't?" Said Dimitri, remembering their first conversation.

"Good," said Gino, "then meet me at the RedBar downtown for the happy hour."

"I'll be there," said Dimitri, excited about the job opportunity and curious to see what he would be doing. Considering the kind of money that was being offered Dimitri initially thought that it might have something to do with organized crime. Miami, after all, was famous for its drug smuggling and its money laundering banks.

At the RedBar, however, Gino assured Dimitri that he had nothing to worry about, that he didn't do business with the South American cartels.

Feeling relieved, Dimitri then asked Gino to describe the job.

"Well, I'm a contract killer for a group of businessmen who are paying me to eliminate whoever they want to eliminate."

"You're a what?"

"A hitman, to put it bluntly."

"And you want me to kill someone?" Asked Dimitri.

"No, I do the killing," said Gino, "you're just my assistant. Still want the job?"

"Absolutely," said Dimitri, "so long as I don't have to kill anyone."

"I give you my word," said Gino, "you won't have to."

Still, Dimitri was curious. Who were these businessmen, he thought, and why did they have this laundry list of South Floridians that they wanted to kill.

"Do you know why these businessmen are murdering people?" Dimitri asked Gino.

"No," said Gino, "people are murdered all the time in Miami and what's more it's none of your business."

"OK," said Dimitri, "but I'm still curious."

"That's your problem," said the Italian.

"Of course," said Dimitri, thinking that if he wanted the job and the money he'd have to stop with the questions and keep his mouth shut.

The Italian remained true to his word. Dimitri never had to kill anyone and every time he went out on a job with Gino ten thousand dollars were automatically deposited on Dimitri's bank account. All together Gino had called Dimitri four times in less than a month, which was great. He was earning a lot of money, but given that ten days had passed from the last time he had heard from the Italian he was beginning to think that Gino didn't need his services anymore.

"Oh well," he said to himself, "nothing lasts forever." And he decided that if the Italian wasn't going to call him then he might as well go to the Clevelander and see if he could find the girl who he'd been obsessing about that day. But then his phone rang and it was the Italian.

"Dimitri?" said Gino.

"Speaking," said Dimitri.

"I've got another easy job for you. Are you ready?"

"When do we go?" Asked Dimitri.

"Now," said the Italian.

"Give me five minutes," said Dimitri.

"We meet at my place," said the Italian, "And bring your Glock. This time it's going to be different."

"No problem, boss," said Dimitri, just before the Italian hung up.

He took the Venetian Causeway to Miami Beach and from there he drove down to a condominium that had a good view of Government Cut and the Gulf Stream. Dimitri liked this area of the city. The Clevelander was nearby and many of the other bars that he frequented. Perhaps, he thought, one of these days when he'd earned enough he'd be able to buy one of those apartments in the condo where the Italian lived. After all, this was the United States, a country of opportunity and very different from his native Russia.

~~~

Gino came out of the condo's underground parking in a Red Lamborghini Huracan.

"Leave your car in the parking," said Gino, "we're going to take mine to Key West."

"Sounds good," said Dimitri and after he had parked his car he walked out of the garage and sat down in the passenger seat of the Lamborghini.

"Nice car," said Dimitri, "where did you get it?"

"I picked it up for next to nothing about a year ago."

"Seriously?" Asked Dimitri.

"I guess you could say it was part of a business deal."

"Sweet," said Dimitri, as he listened to Gino go on about the car. It was a marvel of Italian engineering.

"Fast and light, with excellent handling, this baby was made for speed," said Gino.

"Awesome," said Dimitri. But because the engine couldn't show its potential on the way down to Key West, due to the speed limit, Gino shifted to fourth gear just once and that was when they were going over the Seven Mile Bridge. The torque and the horse power of this car were insane and Dimitri asked Gino why he even bothered getting the car considering that in Florida it was something of a wasted engine.

"It's true," said Gino, "but as I told you I got it for cheap from a client who needed my services but who didn't have the money to pay me, so he gave me his car."

"Well, that's different," said Dimitri, "I thought you guys only accepted cash or its equivalent."

"Normally, we don't accept anything else, but he had the car and I didn't want to lose him as a client, so I said we'll do a trade."

"And that was the end of that?"

"Pretty much, I did what he wanted done and he gave me the keys."

"And what about these businessmen that you're working for now," asked Dimitri, "will they be giving you a car, too?"

"No," said Gino, "no cars this time, just bitcoin."

"I see."

"A quick job, bang, bang and more bitcoin for me and cash for you on your account. Super easy, super quick. Nothing to worry about, you'll see."

Dimitri wasn't worried, not exactly. He had already seen Gino kill four M.D.s, all of them men, and so he knew what to expect. They would trail their next target and when they were close enough Gino would finish the job. There had never been any difficult moments with these M.D.s. They all died without understanding that they were about to be killed. These were quiet executions, with Gino using a suppressor and all you heard was a kind of muted clack when he pulled the trigger on his Beretta Px4 Storm. That and the thud of the victim's body when it hit the ground.

When they arrived in Key West Gino parked the Lamborghini next to the B&B he'd rented on Simonton Street. It was close to the rum distillery and Sloppy Joe's. and at ten p.m. the island was literally packed with tourists, most of them from the cruise ship that had docked on pier B near Mallory Square.

"It's not going to be easy to locate our guy with all these people, don't you think?" Said Dimitri.

"On the contrary, I know exactly where he'll be."

"And how did you manage that?"

"I asked him," said Gino.

"Yeah, sure, just like that," said Dimitri, laughing, "You just walked up to him in Miami and said hey, where you going to be this weekend."

"Don't be silly," said Gino, "I called him and then I pretended to be a Pfizer sales rep. I told him that we were coming out with a new mRNA cancer vaccine and that we wanted his name on the in-house research paper that we created for the drug."

"And he believed you?"

"Why shouldn't he? That sort of stuff happens all the time in his line of work. Plus he knew he wouldn't be doing this for free."

"So we don't need to track him down I'm guessing," said Dimitri.

"Not at all," said Gino, "He's waiting for us at Sloppy Joe's with a colleague from the hospital where he works."

"Nice, you going to shoot them in the bar?"

"Jesus, Dimitri," said Gino, "you really can be stupid sometimes with these jokes of yours."

"Sorry, boss, couldn't help it."

"No, we're going to have a couple of drinks and when we finish with Sloppy Joe's we'll walk across the street to Captain Tony's and from there maybe to The Green Parrot for more drinks. Does that meet with your approval?" Said Gino.

"Sounds like fun, but are you sure we're here for work?"

"Well you can't come to Key West and not take in some of the cultural watering holes, don't you think?"

"I guess not," said Dimitri, as they walked in through the saloon doors of Sloppy Joe's.

"There they are," said Gino, pointing to the M.D. and his colleague who were sitting up at the bar.

"I see the guy at the bar but where's his colleague?" Dimitri asked.

"Right next to him."

"But that's a woman," said Dimitri.

"Indeed she is."

"Another M.D.?" asked Dimitri.

"No, she's a nurse."

"She's cute," said Dimitri.

"Well, lucky you. You can strike up a conversation with her, if you want."

"For how long?" Said Dimitri.

"Hell if I know," said Gino, "depends on if she likes you, I guess."

Dimitri thought that it was all very strange compared to the other jobs, but he didn't say anything. He was going to get paid his ten thousand no matter what happened.

He looked at the nurse again up at the bar and she turned and waved at him. She had curly red hair and was wearing a pair of ripped jeans and a loose white linen blouse. The M.D. was wearing a blue t-shirt that he'd picked up at the bar and a pair of khaki colored shorts. As soon as he saw Gino and Dimitri he got off his stool and shook hands with them. The nurse stayed where she was.

Once they were all seated at the bar they started ordering drinks, a round of mojitos to start off with, followed by a round of daiquiris. The mood was relaxed, just the way Gino wanted it to be. And he and the M.D. talked about the fake research paper and the fifty thousand that the pharmaceutical company would pay him for the use of his name and his prestige.

Dimitri chatted with the nurse. Her name was Jessica Hernandez and she worked in the E.R. at Jackson Memorial in Miami.

Dimitri said that Miami was a great city and asked her if she had been there for long.

"No," she told him, "just a couple of months."

"And you?" She asked.

"Three years," he said.

"And you also work for Pfizer?" She asked.

"No, I'm just here with my friend."

"I see," she said.

Dimitri then asked her, after another round of daiquiris was ordered if she and the M.D. were an item.

"You mean like boyfriend and girlfriend?"

"Something like that," said Dimitri, and she told him no, they were just friends.

Dimitri was happy to hear it. He was having a great time talking to Jessica and wondered how the evening was going to end considering that this was a job and that Gino was being paid to kill her friend and that legally speaking he would be an accomplice to this murder. Indeed, the fact that he had even bothered to ask her if she was going out with the M.D. was ridiculous. Maybe it was just the drinks and her beauty that had given him the courage to ask that question, or maybe it had nothing to do with the drinks. Perhaps, just for a moment, he had forgotten who he was and what he did for a living. Still, even if he had forgotten for a moment who he was, that didn't change anything. Work was work and nothing had ever been given to him for free. Nor was this woman an exception, no matter how pretty she was, no matter how much he wanted her.

And then, almost to emphasize that fact, Gino told everyone in their group that it was time to go to the Green Parrot. The M.D. wanted more to drink and a place where he could dance with his colleague and there was no better locale for that than the Green Parrot.

There were two bands that night playing at the Green Parrot and when they arrived the second band had just started their set. They were a heavy metal group from Austin, Texas and very loud. The M.D., being Gino's guest of honor and his target had first dibs on the nurse. Dimitri and Gino stood by the bar drinking their gin tonics and watching the couple as they danced.

"They look good together, don't you think?" Said Gino.

"Not really," said Dimitri, "I mean, she looks stunning, but he's kinda fat."

"Sounds like you've got a crush," said Gino, smiling.

"No crush, just answering your question," said Dimitri.

After the first song the M.D. walked back to the bar and Dimitri got to dance with Jessica. She seemed surprised to see him standing so close to her and he asked her "do you mind?"

"Not at all," she told him. Then they danced together for two songs and he was even able to move his hands down her hips and she didn't object. Perhaps, he fantasized, tonight would not turn out to be just another easy job, but something more. But back at the bar Gino and the M.D. had other plans. They were going down to the Southernmost Point marker and were taking their most recent round of drinks with them. Dimitri knew that if he followed them then the nurse would know that he was a killer, too, and that would be the end of any chances he had with her. On the other hand, if he walked away with her not only would he not be paid, but there was a good chance that Gino would kill him along with the M.D.

"So, are you two coming?" Gino asked, as he handed them their drinks.

"Sure," said Dimitri, as he looked at Jessica. She gave him a kiss, and smiled.

"This is fun," she said.

"The night is young," agreed Gino, "and we've got a long way to go till sunrise."

At the Southernmost Marker everything was quiet and Gino asked the M.D. and the nurse if they wanted a photo/souvenir of their trip to Key West.

The M.D. said yes while the nurse said that she wanted Dimitri in it, too.

"No, I think it's better to have just you and the doctor. Afterwards we can take other pics."

Dimitri didn't say anything, but he knew what was about to happen and this time he wanted no part in it.

"Stand closer together," said Gino to the M.D. and the nurse, and they did as they were told.

"Like this?" said the nurse, putting her arm around the M.D.

"Perfect," he told her, as he held his iPhone in his left hand and quietly pulled the Px4 out of his right hand pocket.

"Smile," he said, as he shot the M.D. in the forehead. The doctor fell backwards against the Southernmost Marker while the nurse started to scream and run away.

"Dimitri, shoot her before we lose her," said Gino.

"No," he said, pointing his Glock at Gino and pulling the trigger. It hit Gino in his chest killing the Italian on impact.

"Fuck it," said Dimitri, "I'm out of here." And he started to walk back to where the Lamborghini was parked. The keys were in his pocket and tomorrow he'd start looking for another job.

* * *

About The Authors

1.

Robert Coburn is originally from Norfolk, Virginia. After high school in Norfolk, he spent three years in the US Army as a helicopter crew chief stationed in Berlin, Germany. He returned home to attend college at Richmond Professional Institute (Now VCU) in Richmond, Virginia, where he earned a Bachelor of Science degree in Advertising. He also met his wife in Richmond while a student there.

Coburn has worked at major advertising agencies in New York and Los Angeles. His ads have won top awards both nationally and internationally. He is an instrument rated commercial pilot and plays saxophone. He and his wife now live in Carmel, California.

2.

Bill Craig is the best-selling author of more than 60 novels spread across the genres from mystery to pulp to science fiction to westerns. Bill is best known for his Marlow Key West mysteries and his Mitch Cooper mysteries. Bill often likes to say that it only took him 34 years to become an overnight success. And when introducing himself he adds that he kills people for a living... at least in his books.

3.

Shirrel Rhoades is a writer, critic, filmmaker, former college professor, art collector, and publishing consultant. For more than two decades, he and his wife shared their historic classic temple revival style house in Key West with assorted dogs, cats, and a surrogate daughter.

4.

David Beckwith is a three-generation native of Greenville, Mississippi, with a BBA and an MBA from Ole Miss. His parents owned an independent cash commodity trading firm which also cleared securities trades through Goodbody & Co. David spent 40 years in the securities business, the first half of his career with Bache & Co. and its successors, the second half with Morgan Stanley. He retired as a Senior Vice President with approximately $500 million in responsibilities. For 25 years he has served as an adjunct professor at five different universities.

His first book was a narrative nonfiction work published by the University of Alabama Press in 2009 entitled A New Day In The Delta. The Mississippi Institute of Arts and Letters chose it as the runner-up for nonfiction book of the year. The book is often compared to Pat Conroy's The Water Is Wide.

5.

Randolph W.B. Becker has spent his professional career as a Unitarian Universalist Minister and a spiritual adventurer. He has taught at several colleges and theological schools and had one of the first podcasts on a religious theme as the Internet developed. When pressed for a definition, he claims to be a "spiritual humanist."

Dr. Becker is an inveterate traveling who always seeks to be more a temporary resident than a tourist. You will most often find him on public transit, eating at neighborhood restaurants, finding what you do when you get lost, and braving barely-known languages to converse with newly-found friends over a glass of red wine.

6.

G. Steven McMillan is an associate professor at the Abington campus of Penn State University. Prior to joining academia, Steve worked in accounting and real estate in the Philadelphia area. He has received four Fulbright awards that have taken him to Finland, Belgium, and Malta twice. An avid traveler, he has visited over 30 countries.

7.

Howard Lowell Osterman collected a few rejection slips from popular magazines before deciding he preferred the steady salary of a staff writing position with a newspaper. That led to other "writing gigs" with magazines and book publishers. "A good living," Osterman tells it. "But in my spare time I kept cranking out sensational novels and short stories. My dirty little secret, I call them, usually working under pseudonyms to avoid conflicts with employers looking for a pound of flesh." He has lived in New York, Chicago, and Daytona. He enjoys watching old film noir movies. He hopes one day to write a screenplay.

8.

Renee Kumor was a stay-at-home mom for several years developing a personal ethic of community service. Through the years as her children aged, she became active in the political and non-profit life of the community. She began writing a political opinion column for the local newspaper, but retired from writing when she announced her candidacy for local political office. After eight years as a county commissioner, she returned to non-profit service and began writing a monthly column for the newspaper on non-profit board service and management issues. Renee has been married to her husband for more than half a century.

9.

Barthélemy Banks is the nom de plume of a former supervisor for a publishing company that was secretly backed by the CIA. He spent a number of years in the Bahamas where he rubbed elbows with spies, smugglers, international bankers, and reclusive millionaires. Today, he lives on a remote island, where he finds it safe to write about the clandestine world he knows so well.

10.

Jonathan Woods is the author of five pulp noir crime books. His story collection, *Bad Juju & Other Tales of Madness and Mayhem* ("Hallucinatory, hilarious, imaginative noir."—*New York Magazine*) was a featured book at the 2010 Texas Book Festival in Austin and won a 2011 Spinetingler Award for Best Crime Short Story Collection. His other books are:

• *A Death in Mexico*: "Captures that same blend of bleakness and corruption that drives Orson Welles' film noir *Touch of Evil*."— Booklist;

• *Phone Call from Hell and Other Tales of the Damned*: "Cleverly written and deeply, often hilariously, twisted."—Booklist;

• *Kiss the Devil Good Night*: "A frenzied and sprawling masterpiece."—Jon Bassoff; and

• *Hog Wild*: "Awild glorious ride and a fantastic feast of storytelling...Mixing the gothic with the surreal, the western with pulp."—Ken Bruen.

His stories have appeared in *Dallas Noir*, *Murder in Key West #1* and *#2* and other crime fiction anthologies and websites. A former Key West resident, he now divides his time between Dallas and Galveston, Texas.

Bonus.

John Patrick Hemingway is author of *Strange Tribe: A Family Memoir*, which examines the complex relationship between his father Dr. Gregory Hemingway and his grandfather, Nobel Laureate Ernest Hemingway. After studying history and Italian at U.C.L.A., he moved to Italy, then to Spain. He now makes his home in Jacksonville, Florida.

Thank you for reading.
Please review this book. Reviews
help others find Absolutely Amazing eBooks and
inspire us to keep providing these marvelous tales.
If you would like to be put on our email list
to receive updates on new releases,
contests, and promotions, please go to
AbsolutelyAmazingEbooks.com and sign up.

For sales, editorial information, subsidiary rights information
or a catalog, please write or phone or e-mail
AbsolutelyAmazingEbooks
Manhanset House
Shelter Island Hts., New York 11965-0342, US
Tel: 212-427-7139
www.AbsolutelyAmazingEbooks.com
bricktower@aol.com
www.IngramContent.com

For sales in the UK and Europe please contact our distributor,
Gazelle Book Services
White Cross Mills
Lancaster, LA1 4XS, UK
Tel: (01524) 68765 Fax: (01524) 63232
email: jacky@gazellebooks.co.uk